ANGEL'S INTUITION

Liz Borino

A NineStar Press Publication

Published by NineStar Press
P.O. Box 91792,
Albuquerque, New Mexico, 87199 USA.
www.ninestarpress.com

Angel's Intuition

Printed in the USA
First Edition
October, 2018

Print ISBN: 978-1-949340-93-8

Also available in eBook, ISBN: 978-1-949340-88-4

Warning: This book contains sexually explicit content, which may only be suitable for mature readers, and scenes of captivity and torture, and references to violent death.

Chapter One

JULY 2013, LANGLEY, VIRGINIA

CIA Agent Aaron Collins pushed his shoulders together as he strode through the hallway to his supervisor Mick Keller's office and rapped on the door. As if he'd been waiting for him, Keller swung it open. "Come in, Collins, come in. Have a seat. Can I get you a drink?"

"No, thank you, sir," Aaron replied, shifting in the hard, wooden chair. His boss wrung his hands as he circled his large desk. "Is everything all right?" *Clearly not*, he answered himself. Bosses tended not to call emergency meetings on Friday afternoons to discuss the company's upcoming party.

Keller sat behind his desk and adjusted his glasses. "I need you to brief Foster on the POW situation in Afghanistan. The two of you are switching cases."

Aaron blinked. "My team and I have been working with the military on that mission for months. We're three weeks from deployment."

"Yes, Foster will assume your leadership role."

"Foster? He's a paper pusher!"

"Collins." Keller's voice held a warning.

Yeah, God forbid the agency admits the truth about the competence of their employees. "Sir, he really is not qualified."

"He will be once you brief him. We need you here, Collins," Keller told him.

Aaron tilted his head to the side. "Why do you need a field agent here?"

"You're one of our best."

"And...you're afraid to send me because you have reason to doubt safety?"

"It is a rather volatile situation," Keller hedged.

Of course, it's volatile! The fucking enemies have our men! "What aren't you telling me?"

Keller shook his head. "It wasn't my decision."

"Well, whose decision was it? Have you thought of calling them an idiot?"

"Not all of us have your finesse."

"I'm going there, or you need to give me a reason that I can't, beyond the stuffed shirt above you said so," Aaron said.

Keller removed his glasses and massaged his eyes. "No, that's all the reason either one of us requires. Your job is here for the next three months."

"I have the most information about this mission." Even as Aaron spoke, he knew the battle was over.

"None of us know very much." He sighed. "I'm sorry."

So am I. "Can I still get updates?"

"You know we can't." Keller paused, then added, "He'll be all right, Collins."

They weren't talking about Foster's competence anymore. Now, Keller referred to Aaron's husband, Jordan, an army captain also assigned to this mission. "Of course, he will. I only wish I could help."

"You'll help by training Foster," Keller replied.

Right. "Is there anything else, sir?"

"No, you may go home."

"Thank you." Aaron stood, shook Keller's hand, and walked out of the building after grabbing his messenger bag. He ducked into his car and leaned his head back on the seat. He dialed Jordan's cell.

"Hey, Angel, you done already?" Jordan asked. The perkiness in his voice signaled he did not get the same news today.

And like magic, the sound of Jordan's nickname for him eroded the edges of Aaron's bad mood. "Yep, you?"

"Two beers in at home," Jordan responded. "I've got dinner started."

"See, now I think you're vying to steal my nickname." Aaron started the ignition and put his foot on the brake.

"Never happen. You okay?" Jordan asked.

"Uh…do we have anything stronger than beer, or should I stop?"

"Oh, boy." Jordan's tone grew serious. "We have whiskey, if that will do."

Best you can get in the US. Aaron released a breath. "That'll work. Love you."

"Love you too." Jordan ended the call, and Aaron began the twenty-minute trek home to Maryland.

WHEN AARON PULLED up in front of their house, Jordan set his sweatpants on the couch and closed the curtains. As soon as Aaron walked in, he stepped into Jordan's embrace and kissed the top of his head, which reached Aaron's shoulder. Not because Jordan was short, but at almost seven feet, Aaron eclipsed everyone. Jordan loved having the ability to wrap Aaron's pale, slender frame completely in his dark, muscled arms.

"You feel perfect there," Aaron murmured.

"We always did fit together. Why don't you get changed?"

Aaron nodded, but before he could go up the stairs, Jordan pointed to the sweats on the couch. "You are too good to me." Aaron kissed him quickly.

"What happened?" Jordan asked as Aaron undressed.

"Know Foster?" Aaron gathered his suit in a bundle and tossed it in the laundry room on the way to the kitchen.

"The South Korea specialist?" Jordan clarified, and Aaron nodded. "Sure, what about him?" He gave Aaron another peck on the lips after he sank onto the bar stool at the kitchen counter.

As Jordan made his way to the stove to stir the sauce, he noted Aaron crossing and uncrossing his legs and clanking the ice in his whiskey sour against the glass.

"He's taking my place in the POW mission," Aaron answered his unspoken musing.

Jordan dropped a metal spoon into the skillet. "Fuck! Shit!" He licked his fingers after each try to get it out.

"Tongs." Aaron laughed and handed them to him.

After successfully extracting the spoon, Jordan set the stove to simmer and faced Aaron. "He's doing what, now?"

"My reaction exactly," Aaron replied.

"Did he say why?" Jordan asked. "Wait. How's garlic bread sound?"

"Amazing."

"Make yourself useful. There's fresh bread in the drawer," Jordan told him.

Aaron rolled his eyes but kept his smile. "As for why, Keller started to offer bullshit about it being too dangerous for me, but when I pressed, he admitted it was not his decision."

"That much I believe." Jordan shook his head. "Probably the new Director of Military Affairs. He seems to be pulling strings."

"Any idea who it is? Can we egg his house or something?"

"I don't know who he is, but I can tell you this: evasiveness is not winning him any fans," Jordan answered, not adding how much he'd like to egg the man's house.

"Evasiveness? You mean hiding his identity?"

"I actually care less about that than the decisions he's making. I don't get the feeling he's telling us everything he knows."

"Why should he? People on his level make the decisions and hand them down. They don't have to justify."

"Most people in his position would explain important decisions to the officers acting them out." Not that the officers would necessarily pass that information down to the soldiers, but they would understand, which meant the people below them would have reason to trust them. "Does Foster know anything about the POW situation?"

Aaron nudged Jordan out of the way to put the bread in the oven. "Foster doesn't know a damn thing about the Middle East."

"So, how is it less dangerous to send him?" Jordan asked, leaning against the counter.

"I'm supposed to brief him on the information I have." Aaron huffed a breath.

Jordan blinked. "Fifteen years of training on Middle Eastern politics?"

"No, just what's in the file."

"Which gives him approximately 30 to 40 percent of the needed information."

"If that," Aaron confirmed. "What can I do? Keller claims it's out of his hands, so it's sure as hell out of mine."

Jordan poured the pasta into the boiling water. "You can't do anything."

After a pause, Aaron asked, "Can you?"

Chewing on his lip as he watched the noodles jump in the bubbles, Jordan replied, "Not for this mission. Someone qualified should be there. But no reason I have to stay beyond it."

Aaron touched his shoulder. "You're talking about desertion?"

"No. That would ruin us. I'll resign my commission at the end of this deployment." He absently stirred the pasta as his mind whirled around the words he never thought he'd think, much less say. After a few minutes of silence, Jordan looked back at his husband. "No response?"

"Trying to figure out how much you had to drink."

Jordan smiled. "I'm not drunk."

"Then...why?"

Once he'd removed the bread from the oven, Jordan plated their dinner. "Because I can't protect the members of my platoon, civilians, or myself without supportive leaders." If this had been the first or second time a higher-up played roulette with the lives of his soldiers, Jordan woulds take less extreme action. Request a meeting, ask for reasoning, maybe, but at this point, he knew he'd only get some version of "it is the way it is." He didn't need to hear it again.

"Okay," Aaron said, sitting down at the counter and gesturing Jordan over.

"Okay? I tell you I'm changing our lives...and all you say is okay?"

Aaron kissed his cheek. "That, and you better not let Foster's incompetence keep us from jumping out of a plane when you come home." As he bit into the pasta, Aaron added, "I don't know what you're planning to do when you're done, but I'd approve of you staying home to have dinner on the table every night when I get off work."

"Oh, would you?" Jordan turned Aaron's head to the side and brought their lips together between bites. "I failed on that front today."

"Eh, you'll learn. Besides, I was early," Aaron responded. "Any ideas about next steps?"

Jordan exhaled. Up until a few years ago, he'd fully intended to be a military officer for the rest of his working life. But with the disillusionment of regime shake-ups, the thought of a new path sounded better and better. "Maybe I'll go back to school for my PhD in social work."

"Yeah? Then what?"

Draining his beer, Jordan said, "I would like to help improve the foster system. Give the kids who don't get adopted some sort of support." He had seen too many of them pushed into the front line of the army because they had no one to show them other options. And an unfortunate number of those enlistees came home in a wood box with no one to mourn the loss. With an uncertain, yet too dark, ethnicity, Jordan easily could have been one of them. He shook the thought away and glanced at Aaron, who stared at him. "I know it's a pay cut…"

Aaron waved him off. "And you know I don't give a shit. I care only that you're happy."

"Doesn't bother you at all?"

"That you'll be in less danger? Somehow I'll get over it." Aaron rested his head on Jordan's shoulder. "But you're reinforcing my earlier point that you deserve the nickname Angel, not me."

Jordan kissed his head and whispered, "No, you're my angel. Nothing will change that."

They spent the rest of the night talking and making plans.

Chapter Two

JULY 2013, BETHESDA, MARYLAND

Aaron inhaled the mixture of pine, leather, cherry blossoms, and the freshness of his husband, Jordan. The cherry blossom scent drifted through the cracked window letting in the July air, and the cruel light streaming through the window implored his eyes to open. Aaron resisted because as soon as he acknowledged the morning, he would have to be responsible. Get up, put on clothes, and take Jordan to the airport where he'd board a plane and disappear for three months. Jordan's shortest deployment to date, and the only one Aaron would have no part in.

"Last time," Jordan whispered, as though reading Aaron's thoughts.

"Mm, we hope," Aaron answered, kissing the hair adorning Jordan's chest. He tapped his fingers down Jordan's arm and traced the tattoo of an open parachute with strings attached to the words "My Angel." It reflected Aaron's tattoo of a dog tag inscribed with "My Hero."

"Hope?" Jordan grinned and rolled on top of him. "What's to hope?"

Aaron wrapped his arms around Jordan's waist and brought him down for a hug. "Hope the army doesn't find you so invaluable that—"

Jordan cut him off with a kiss. "I was making a request. I want you one last time before we have to get out of bed. That requires agreement, not hope."

"When have I ever not agreed?" Aaron ran his hands down Jordan's back and cupped his ass. At Jordan's contemplative expression, he clarified, "When illness or injury wasn't present?"

"I'm out," Jordan replied.

Without much effort, Aaron flipped Jordan onto his back and pinned his shoulders to the bed. "Then I'll be in." He grabbed the lube from the nightstand. "Did you leave that out on purpose last night?"

"No, but putting it in the drawer would have been wasted effort." Jordan slid his legs apart so Aaron could kneel between them. "God, Angel, you're perfect like that."

Angel. Aaron smiled at Jordan's name for him. He'd started using it the night they'd met, eleven years ago.

"Do I want to see inside your head?" Jordan asked, preventing him from falling into the memory.

"Can you reach it?"

"Sure, if you put it to good use," he threw back.

Aaron bent down and captured Jordan's lips. He yearned to grasp the moment and never let it go.

"Fuck me, damn it!" Jordan growled after they separated, and bit Aaron's neck.

"Hey..." Aaron's shiver weakened the protest. "No marks. I have to work today. Besides, where's the romance in fucking?"

Jordan's eyes softened with his answer. "My love, would you please lube your cock up and stick it in my ass? I desire to connect with you on the most intimate level while we both get off."

Aaron chuckled as he acquiesced with Jordan's request. His laughter ceased as Jordan's slick channel hugged him. "Oh."

"Yes!" Jordan wrapped his legs around Aaron's ass, urging him on. They thrust together, alternating rhythms from slow and deep to fast and needy. Aaron couldn't tell where one stopped and the other began, especially once Jordan shot his cream between them, sealing their bodies. "Angel?"

"Hmm?" Aaron lifted his gaze to meet Jordan's brown eyes.

"Last time."

Aaron offered one more smile and kiss. "No more time, love."

Jordan shook his head. "That was a promise."

Aaron allowed the words to fill his heart as he pulled his husband into the bathroom for a shower.

YEAH, AARON TYPED on the military spouse forums. *Watching J's camouflage fade into the crowd of people at the airport damn near killed me. How do you all handle the separation and worry year after year?*

"That does not look like CIA work, Agent Collins," a man standing over Aaron said. "My name is Major General Troy Hart, the new Associate Director for Military Affairs."

Shit. I'm on my new boss' bad side on his first day. Wait. Didn't Jordan believe the ADMA was responsible for Foster taking my place? Aaron stood and shook the man's hand. He tried not to smirk as Troy took a step backward and raised his eyebrows at Aaron's height. His superior was shorter than the average man, with graying hair and a soft build.

"Guess I can see why you aren't on the covert field team."

"No, sir, I don't blend in very easily. And if it's all right, I was posting on a forum during my lunch break," Aaron explained.

"No," Troy responded. "That is absolutely not all right. You should be away from your desk during lunch."

"I'm fine with a sandwich and a different computer."

"That was an order, Officer Collins. You've had enough stress today to earn a lunch in the cafeteria."

"Earn, sir? Here I thought lunch in the cafeteria was a punishment," Aaron joked. The alternative was for him to demand to know why someone was giving him orders on how to spend his lunch break.

Troy laughed, which only served to irritate Aaron more. "Fair assessment, agent. I'll buy. And it's not necessary to call me 'sir.'"

"I use 'sir' for people I respect."

"We haven't known each other long enough for me to have earned your respect."

No shit.

"So, why don't you start with calling me 'Troy' while we work on fixing that?"

"Let me shut down my computer."

"Great!" Troy said with way more enthusiasm than lunch in the cafeteria warranted.

As Aaron shut down his computer, he received an instant message from Jordan. Damn. He would much rather stay and chat with his husband than eat soggy carrots in the cafeteria.

Hey, babe, you in the air? Aaron quickly typed.

With a screaming toddler a row back. I miss home already, Jordan replied.

Aaron threw a glance over his shoulder to find Troy leaning in close to one of the female interns. *Yeah? Well, I promise it'll be here waiting for you.*

Can't wait. Try to miss me.

I'll do my best. Get some sleep. I have to go to lunch with the new MA boss, Aaron typed.

All right. Tell me about him later.

I love you. Be safe.

The only danger I face right now is going deaf from the toddler. I'll call when I land. And I love you too, Angel. More than you know.

Jordan's screen name faded, indicating he had signed off, and Aaron released a breath.

Angel was not a name most people would have attributed to Aaron when he'd met Jordan at a mixer for CIA interns and low-level army officers more than eleven years ago...

Chapter Three

ELEVEN YEARS EARLIER, WASHINGTON, DC

"You look constipated," Wendy, a rising star in the CIA internship, commented to Aaron.

"How do you know I'm not?" he threw back.

"You'd be eating fruit, if past experience holds true."

Aaron stared at her. "How would you know…?"

"Last week, I saw you take an ex-lax and eat berries with your breakfast. Since you don't have an eating disorder, I knew you weren't purging," she explained, but then scrunched up her face. "You don't have an eating disorder, do you? Sound mental health is so important for the psychologically intense work we'll be doing."

"Wendy, that's creepy. Please, if you must pay attention to people's digestive habits, don't tell them." Aaron shook his head. "I have a final tomorrow, and I'm stuck at this mandatory meeting with—"

"Some of the *finest* leaders our country has to offer," Wendy interrupted, licking her lips.

"It's not speed dating."

"Well, it isn't a meeting. Do you see a boardroom?"

"Nope, I see a bar where I can't drink. Besides, you can't date military officers and work in military affairs," Aaron reminded her, finishing his Coke. Technically you could, but the bosses preferred you not.

"We can't *marry* officers. Big difference. And if you practice holding your alcohol, you could manage a drink or two at work functions."

Aaron had to chuckle. Alcohol tolerance was not at the top of his list of things to improve on. Study skills? Sure. Time management? Certainly wouldn't hurt. He turned to answer her, but she had already caught the attention of a soon-to-be-officer. Even with the increase of women in the military and the CIA, they were grossly outnumbered, and many of the men flocked to the few who came to these events.

"She's not interested in him," a man next to Aaron said.

Aaron turned to find a well-built, tan-skinned Korean man—no, wait, not only Korean, too dark for that. African American? Maybe. His name tag read Jordan Collins. "She'll be interested in the next drink offer. Why? Hoping she'd pay attention to you?"

"No, I prefer the tall blond type." Jordan swept his gaze over Aaron.

Meeting his eyes to confirm his intention, Aaron leaned down and whispered, "Should you be so open? I could be homophobic. If I was offended enough to report you, you would be facing some grim consequences."

"You're not. See—" Jordan made a show of reading his name tag. "—Aaron Larson, you have no more interest in that very attractive woman than I do. And yet, I got your first smile of the evening." He took a breath and continued, "Besides, if you were homophobic, you would have recoiled when I stepped into your personal space. Instead, you leaned closer."

"All right, you win for gaydar. I'm Aaron, obviously. Do you go by Jordan?" Aaron held out his hand, which Jordan shook.

"I do, but I must say, Aaron does not suit you," Jordan commented and took a slug of his beer.

"No? And you know me well enough to make that judgment?"

Jordan tilted his head to the side. "When the light hit your spiked blond hair, it glowed like a halo. Angel suits you much better."

"That may be the worst pickup line ever." In spite of himself, Aaron's face flushed and his heart sped up.

"You don't believe that."

Aaron shook his head. "But I do believe you could get in trouble if someone else were to take issue with…our shared interest. Don't Ask, Don't Tell is serious business."

"You're right. Why don't we get out of here?"

Aaron should be studying if he wasn't here, and Jordan should not be seen with an openly gay man while wearing his army uniform. For no logical reason, Aaron said, "Sure, I'll meet you at the diner two blocks away."

An easy smile grew on Jordan's face as he replied, "See you soon, Angel."

JULY 2013, LANGLEY, VIRGINIA

Aaron jumped as Troy tapped his shoulder. "If you wanted to ditch me, you probably should have done a better job of hiding," Troy told him with a smile.

"Thought we established that I don't hide well," Aaron replied. "Do we still have time for lunch?"

"I will be happy to provide any documentation your direct supervisor needs." Troy waited while Aaron stood and slid his computer into its case, making sure to conceal his face so Troy missed him rolling his eyes. "Is that necessary?" Troy asked, gesturing to the messenger bag.

"To keep my sanity, yes. I'm never without my netbook. Trust me, I'll be much less distracted if I have it."

"Is distraction a problem for you?" Troy took two steps for each of Aaron's strides.

Aaron slowed his pace. "Problem implies a negative impact on my life. So, no. What made you transfer from the military to CIA?"

"I hoped for a more stable lifestyle. I've been serving for twenty years."

"Then you retired and joined the CIA?"

"Yes, the associate director position became available around the time I would have been presented the opportunity to retire. It seemed like a sign."

Aaron nodded. "My husband, Jordan, is a big believer in fate, signs, and divine intervention." He liked to work his marital status into early conversations with people to squelch any false hope they might be building about romance. Not that he expected such an interest from someone of Troy's position, but he took the precaution just the same.

"Husband? Oh, you're married to Captain Jordan Collins, aren't you?" Troy said as they reached the cafeteria floor.

"Yes, do you know him?"

Troy led Aaron to the back of the line. "I know of him. He's always been an asset to the army. His leaders will be sad to see his career end."

I won't. "He's going back for his PhD in social work."

"I know. I've been following Captain Collins' career for the past few years." Before Aaron could think too hard about what he'd said, Troy gestured to the glass case. "What do you like?"

"Salad's fine for me, thanks."

"Any chicken or beef on it?"

"I try not to eat cafeteria meat. Never know how it's prepared," Aaron told him.

"CIA doesn't take care of its employees?"

"They try, but I still don't trust many people with my health."

Troy stared at Aaron for a long moment, ordered and paid for their meals, and led him to a table in the corner. "I'm willing to bet it's more than your health you don't trust many people with."

Aaron squinted. "Actually, I minored in biology in college, in case I changed my mind and became a doctor. So, it really is about putting my health in a stranger's hands, no deep psychological meaning."

"Maybe I'm projecting. Sorry. I've been told I do that," Troy said.

"By your wife?"

"Ex-wife and three ex-boyfriends," he replied. "I'm working on it. Anyway, tell me about your family. Who do you have besides Jordan? Any kids?"

Aaron laughed. "No kids. He and I made that agreement when we got married. My mother died when I was a baby, and my dad got remarried to a woman with a son a year later."

"That's great. And Jordan?"

"He was adopted by a fantastic couple who couldn't have children." Aaron picked at his salad. "His mother died two years ago after getting hit by a drunk driver."

"I'm sorry," Troy said.

"Thanks," Aaron replied. "What family do you have?"

"A daughter and a brother. Parents have long since passed away." Troy opened his mouth but shut it when his phone beeped. A smile spread across his face as he read the message. "I apologize, Aaron, but my friend let me know that she got us tickets to the AC/DC reunion concert in September."

"How did she manage that? Those tickets have been sold out since about three minutes after they went on sale."

"Paid the amount of my rent for each. Are you a fan?"

"Not as much as my older brother, Chris. He's such a weirdo that he was actually disappointed he didn't 'get' to wait outside overnight." Aaron left out the fact that he would be joining Chris at the show.

Troy laughed. "Yeah, the internet killed all our fun." He took a breath. "Well, as much as I would like to stay and get to know each other, we should probably go back to work."

Aaron nodded. "Thanks for lunch. It was more interesting than I expected."

"Oh, high praise. Maybe next time, I won't have to work so hard to convince you?"

"Maybe," Aaron conceded. He cleared his tray and followed Troy upstairs to finish their days.

Chapter Four

JULY 2013, KABUL, AFGHANISTAN

Jordan tossed the last of his suitcases on the floor in the bedroom of his condo, a few miles outside of Kabul. As an officer, Jordan was spared living in the barracks, but that did not make his arrangements comfortable. Certainly not home. He shook his head. He could deal for three months. Jordan made the decision to remind himself every day of why he was there, and what he'd be going back to.

He had intended to enlist right out of high school, as his dad had done. But Jordan's father had begged him to go to college through the ROTC program, so he had a chance to implement the changes he dreamed of instead of following the orders of people who did not share his vision. Jordan soon learned that even closer to the top, change from a two-hundred-plus-year-old organization was slow at best. And people at the top of other countries believed in their values as strongly as Americans believed in theirs. So Jordan had to convince them they were wrong. Tomorrow. Tonight, he would talk to Aaron and sleep. He glanced at his phone and decided to wait to call. Aaron wouldn't be home yet anyway.

Jordan chuckled to himself as he thought of the night they first got together...

ELEVEN YEARS EARLIER, WASHINGTON, DC

Even as he entered the diner to find Aaron waiting, Jordan still struggled to believe that he'd persuaded Aaron Larson to leave the mixer by using the worst pickup line ever. But as he'd stood across the room, all he could think was, *Angels should smile. I'm going to see if I can change his mood.* Jordan's gaydar had sharpened as soon as he'd entered the military and hitting on the wrong person could cost him his job.

"Hey, Angel," Jordan said, taking a seat at the booth.

"Are you honestly going to continue calling me that?"

"Is it going to continue making you blush?" Jordan countered, deepening the red in the man's cheeks even further. "I'll stop if it bothers you."

Aaron shook his head. "Doesn't bother me. It is an odd descriptor for someone you only met a half hour ago. Unless you make a habit of judging people by their appearance."

Appearance told more than most people liked to admit. Jordan would get there eventually. "Fair enough. What if we get to know each other a little better and reevaluate if Angel fits you?" Jordan opened the menu.

"Okay. It won't," Aaron told him. "The burgers here are fantastic, if you're a meat eater."

Jordan raised his eyebrow. "Do I look like a vegetarian?"

"Now not only do angels all look the same, but vegetarians, as well?" Aaron threw back.

"*That* has a biological basis. Vegetarians eat less protein, and therefore, build less muscle than people who eat from all the food groups."

"Every single vegetarian in the history of the world consumes less protein than the general population?" Aaron asked.

Jordan raised his hands in surrender. "I need some calories before entering into verbal volleyball." He ordered french fries and a cheeseburger from the waitress. His jaw dropped when Aaron requested a salad. Jordan quickly closed his mouth so as not start another debate, but damn if Aaron wasn't proving Jordan's point about body types by eating salad instead of meat.

"By the way, I'm not a vegetarian. I am selective with what goes in my body," Aaron clarified, seemingly reading Jordan's thoughts.

"Yeah? Good to know."

Aaron rolled his eyes. "You're infuriating."

Jordan smiled. "You like it."

"Why would you say that?"

"Still here, aren't you?"

Releasing a breath, Aaron said, "Yes, yes. What makes you think I'm an angel?"

"What makes you think you're not?" Jordan leaned back to assess the man across from him. He had to ensure he was not pushing too far. But so far, Aaron seemed to be enjoying his annoyance, because no matter what he said, he kept the tiniest smile.

"Do you always answer a question with a question?"

Jordan fused their gazes. "Only when your answer is more important than mine. See, I called you Angel because the light made your hair shine. And...every other time I have seen you, you've been helping someone."

Aaron tilted his head to the side. "What are you talking about? We haven't met before tonight."

"No, but I've seen you around. First time was six weeks ago in the writing center at Georgetown. You were working with a football player to keep his scholarship. Then last week, you stopped a dog from getting hit by a car."

The conversation paused as they thanked the waitress for their drinks. Once she left, Aaron asked, "Have you been stalking me?"

Had he truly been concerned about sitting across from a dangerous stalker, Aaron's voice would have heightened and his body would have stiffened. Neither of those things was the case, so Jordan smiled and replied, "No, I happened to be in the writing center working with a tutor at the same time as you, and I was jogging across the street when you saved the dog. At that point, I would have stopped to introduce myself, but I had a drill sergeant screaming a few paces behind me."

Aaron's gaze darted around the room before he leaned closer and lowered his voice. "Speaking of drill sergeants, we need to discuss you being out with me in your uniform. I never had a closet to come out of, so if you're seen with me, people would have reason to be suspicious."

Jordan caught Aaron's smoldering gray eyes, covered his hand with his own, and took note of the other man's tripping pulse. "Relax. My comrades know. My superiors have guessed. Could the wrong person start trouble? Sure, but my private life has never interfered with my job or schoolwork. It never will."

"So you're telling me you're the exception to the law? Don't Ask, Don't Tell doesn't apply to you?"

"Of course, it does, but the fact is I'm smarter than most people. I can read a room within seconds of walking in. I have never once incurred bullying for my sexuality. I don't hit on men who aren't gay, and I avoid flamboyant men. They would get me in trouble." Jordan moved his hand but kept eye contact. "If I want to get to know someone, I don't let my job stop me. Granted, certain things are more difficult. For example, I can't bring my partners as dates to work events, and it's probably a bad idea to take them on base."

"Do you live on base?" Aaron's expression softened.

"No. I have an apartment in Bethesda, Maryland," Jordan answered. He silently cheered as the hesitancy faded from Aaron's face, but not yet. "You still haven't answered my question."

"What's that?"

"Why do you think you aren't angelic?"

Aaron pushed his fingers through his hair and shook his head. "Because I'm not that innocent."

"Oh, thank God." Jordan grinned, his eyes widening at the food placed in front of him. "Clearly, neither am I. Neither are any of us. And, anyway, if you really want to get philosophical, we can talk about how innocence is relative to experience and perception."

"Why not start with what you enjoy doing?" Aaron poured salad dressing over the crisp lettuce, carrots, tomatoes, and cucumbers.

Jordan studied Aaron's meal. "Didn't the menu say house salads included olives, onions, and cheese?"

"Yes, but I come here a few times a week, so they know my order."

"You bring all the guys you pick up at the bar here?" Jordan asked between bites.

Aaron scowled. "I don't pick guys up at bars, and before you say it, *you* picked *me* up. Now, what do you like to do, besides having circular conversations?"

"Hmm, I play piano, guitar, trumpet, and violin, but in the past few years I've focused on the guitar."

"Why? Are you in a rock band?" Aaron's eyes gleamed at the question.

"Sorry to disappoint, but not since high school. I focused on the guitar because it's more portable than a piano, so I can take it when I move, and it's more versatile than the others."

"I don't know. I'd like to hear a violin version of 'Highway to Hell,'" Aaron responded.

"Never tried it, but I bet it would work with the right bass and drums behind the violin. I can do 'Smoke on the Water' on all my instruments." Jordan chuckled. "Any musical interests for you?"

"I tried a few times growing up, but never had the patience for practicing. I'm more into sports. But not—"

"Basketball," Jordan interrupted. "I figured. You don't have the body type, except your height." He scrutinized the man across from him. Judging by what Jordan could see of his arms and torso, Aaron had sleek, defined muscles. He'd have to take off the man's loosened tie and button-up shirt and black slacks to know for sure. Jordan forcibly removed his mind from the gutter. "I'm going to say...swimming?"

Aaron grinned. "I started when I was five. I do some running, too, but water's always been my passion."

"I like the water, but after a hard workout. What part of the CIA are you hoping to work for after graduation? Or can't you talk about it?"

"I can probably talk about my job as much as you can talk about yours. I'm an intern now, which means I'm getting exposed to all the different branches of the CIA, but I'm most drawn to Military Affairs."

"What group?"

"Command and Coordination for the Middle East. I've studied Middle Eastern politics throughout college."

Crap. Jordan had been afraid of that. But damn if every nerve in his body didn't fire in this man's presence. "I'm Foreign Affairs."

"Ah." Aaron nodded. "We should go home alone

tonight, then."

"Probably." Jordan downed the rest of his drink. Neither man made any attempt to act on his common sense. "Want to hear 'Smoke on the Water'?"

Aaron signaled for the check and replied, "No." He paused long enough for Jordan to consider that he might be engaging his brain after all. "But I would love to hear something original."

"Angel it is," Jordan said as they left the diner.

Chapter Five

JULY 2013, KABUL, AFGHANISTAN

The ringing phone brought Jordan from his memory. "Captain Collins speaking."

"Captain, Colonel Bryant here. How was your flight?" Bryant boomed. The art of speaking in conversational tone was entirely lost on him.

"Fine, sir. I am currently settling into the condo," Jordan replied, angling the phone away from his ear.

"Those condos are wonderful, aren't they? I picked them out myself."

"You made a great selection. Thank you." Jordan assessed the drab coloring and tiny rooms. *Better than the alternatives.*

"Of course! I take care of my officers. You've been told about the meeting tomorrow morning?"

Tomorrow? I thought the meeting was August first... Which would be tomorrow, Jordan thought as he read the schedule. "Yes, sir. I will meet you at 0800 hours in the embassy building."

"Better get there early for check-in, Captain," Colonel Bryant suggested.

"No problem. Have a good night." Jordan waited for the LTC to return the sentiment to hang up. He studied the clock on his phone to translate the time difference between Kabul and Maryland. Six thirty a.m. there. Jordan set up his computer on the bed next to him. After the Windows screen appeared, he keyed in the internet code, then encrypted his IP address, and signed onto Skype. "Hey, Angel," he said when Aaron accepted his video call.

"Hey. How're the digs?" Aaron leaned back on his elbows.

"Everything works."

"That's an improvement from the last deployment. What was it, um, the hot water wasn't quite hot, right?"

"It was plenty hot, but only when it felt like it. Unfortunately, its desires didn't always match with ours," Jordan clarified. The forlorn expression on Aaron's face told him that he was thinking about how while the water didn't work, the last time Jordan was overseas, they were together.

"Tell me something interesting," Aaron requested.

"Nothing interesting here, and honestly, I'd like to keep it that way. Boring deployments are best." A movement in the opposite corner of the room caught Jordan's eye. "Hold on a second." He rushed over to find a camel spider whose abdomen alone spanned eight inches. "Fuck!"

"What's wrong?" Aaron asked over the computer speakers.

"Got a roommate, it seems." Jordan scooped the spider onto a hardcover book and held it away from his body.

"Roommate?" Aaron made a face as Jordan passed the camera with the spider. "Why didn't you kill it?"

"Because then I'd have to clean up spider guts." He opened the window and dumped the spider out. "And they don't die easily."

Aaron shivered. "Check the place before you sleep tonight."

"Fuck that shit. I'm going to buy repellent as soon as I'm finished talking to you." Jordan swept his gaze over the bed and lifted the skirt to survey underneath. "Clear so far." He always took precautions after another soldier had been bitten and ended up in the hospital the last time Jordan was over here. Once he settled back on the bed, Jordan said, "I meant to ask you; who's the new ADMA?"

"Major General Troy Hart."

Jesus Christ. I was right. I'll put money on the fact Hart was the one to take Aaron off the mission. "Seriously? I thought we were done with him." Jordan huffed out a breath.

Aaron blinked. "What's your issue?"

"He's..." *The asshole that almost killed my whole platoon.* "By the book." He finally decided that was appropriate.

"Add pompous to that, and you're describing 99 percent of military officers. I would say one hundred, but we're married," Aaron said. "What makes him different?"

"He just...makes decisions without listening to the people closer to the ground, as you can see by his order to replace you," Jordan told him.

"Are you sure he made that decision? I thought that was just speculation on your part."

"Not 100 percent sure, no, but the major general runs departments, platoons, and everything else very heavy-handedly." At Aaron's questioning expression, Jordan shook his head. "I can't say more. Why were you dealing with him? Isn't he a few levels above you?"

"I don't know. Troy sought me out at my desk during lunch," Aaron explained.

"Troy? You two are on a first-name basis?"

"We had lunch together." Aaron sat up and waved his confusion off. "You are not jealous of someone I had lunch with at work, because that would be ridiculous."

Jordan focused on the ceiling and counted to ten. "Not jealous. Surprised. You tend to avoid superiors whenever possible."

"I figured there was no harm in being nice to him. I need all the recommendations I can get if we're leaving town," Aaron explained. "He likes you."

Jordan ran his palm over his buzz cut and took a second to process. Hart had no reason to like him. "Does he know me?"

"Your reputation precedes you, I guess." Aaron paused and asked, "Is this a problem for you? I'm not invested enough to object to ignoring him."

"No, I don't care who you talk to. I *am* curious why he sought you out. Did he say anything specific about me?"

"He was sad you were resigning, said you were an asset to the army. Same thing everyone else has told you."

Jordan smiled. "Did you tell him that you were not sad?"

"I didn't go into the details I normally would, but I think he got it." Aaron relaxed his posture. "Hey, Jordan?"

"Hmm?"

"I love you," Aaron said.

Jordan's smile eased from amusement to the comfort those words brought. "I love you too, Angel." He stacked two pillows behind him and lay down on them. "I was thinking about the night we met earlier."

"Yeah? Me too." Aaron grinned. "You never did play guitar for me that night."

"If I remember correctly, we were rather busy once we got back to my place. I can play now."

"Mm, I'd love to hear a song before my meeting."

"Didn't you just get home?" Jordan worked to not let his disappointment show.

"Yeah. Dinner meeting."

"That's okay," Jordan reassured him. "I have one in the morning." Which meant another short call.

"Have I told you I hate separate deployments?" Aaron offered a rueful smile.

"Last one," Jordan reminded him and climbed off the bed to grab his guitar. "Any requests?"

Aaron scrunched his face in consideration as he stood to dress. "Surprise me."

Jordan strummed his acoustic guitar, randomly at first while he decided on a song. Soon his fingers moved to the tune of Billy Joel's "You're My Home." Aaron stared at him for a few seconds and sang along with the music. Jordan only sang when he wrote lyrics, but Aaron was quick to learn them because, well, it was better for everyone that Jordan not sing. "You're My Home," a song about a traveler who only needed his lover by his side to be content, was the closest thing Aaron and Jordan had to "their song."

"You're a jerk," Aaron told him, fixing his tie. "But I love you."

"I know. I love you too. Enjoy your meeting. I'll talk to you in the morning before mine."

Jordan shut his laptop when Aaron signed off. He forced himself off the bed to ensure all the windows were sealed. The last thing he wanted was to wake up with spiders biting him. He shuddered at the thought. After completing that task, he settled under the covers for a nap, but the beep of his phone interrupted sleep. He unlocked the screen to find a text message from Aaron.

Eighty-nine days until you're home.

And that was enough to quiet his restless mind.

ELEVEN YEARS EARLIER, BETHESDA, MARYLAND

Jordan's spirits lifted all over again to see Aaron leaning against his Mazda in the parking lot outside of Jordan's apartment. "It's cold," he called, locking his own car.

"Then hurry up and let me inside," Aaron replied with a laugh.

Jordan led him up the outside steps to his second-floor apartment. "How are you not shivering?" he questioned as he unlocked the door, taking in Aaron's lack of a winter coat.

"Have to be outside a lot longer than this to get to the point of shivering."

Swinging the door open, Jordan gestured Aaron inside. "Watch your head."

Aaron laughed again and ducked through the doorway. "That is something you never need to remind me of."

Tossing his keys down, Jordan leaned on the island and swept his gaze over the full length of Aaron's body. He was not used to attraction burning so hot so fast.

"Better have a dollar if you're going to look at me like that."

"Angel, you are worth way more than a dollar." Jordan tugged him closer.

"Is that so?" Aaron said, inches away, breath hot.

Still, Aaron's height prevented Jordan from bridging the distance between their hungry mouths in their current positions. He pushed the books on the island to the lower counter, not caring when they clattered to the floor.

Aaron must have figured out what Jordan was going for, because he lifted him by the waist onto the island and sealed their lips together. "God, Jordan, I want you," he panted between kisses.

Jordan yanked Aaron's shirt over his head, kissed down his neck, and bit his nipples. "You have no idea," Jordan growled.

"Sure about that?" Aaron took Jordan's hand and pressed it to his burgeoning fly. He removed Jordan's uniform shirt, discarding it on the floor with his own.

Mutual attraction confirmed, Jordan hopped off the island and made his way toward his bedroom. "Coming?"

"I hope so."

"Me too." Jordan sat on the bed and said, "Strip for me, please."

"Just gonna watch me?" Aaron asked, his cheeks pinkening.

"Unless it bothers you. I think you're gorgeous with clothes on. Can't wait to see the whole picture."

He had no right to expect compliance, but Aaron popped the button on his black pants and lowered them, along with his boxers. Aaron kicked all his clothes to the side.

"I was right." Jordan brought Aaron between his legs and kissed down his happy trail.

"Perfect positioning."

"Should I use a condom?" Jordan questioned, meeting Aaron's eyes.

Aaron rummaged through his wallet for his test results and handed them to Jordan. "No, I don't usually carry them with me, in case you were curious."

"Knew tonight would be special, huh?" Jordan took his results out of the nightstand drawer.

Squinting, Aaron asked, "Isn't there something better you could be doing with your mouth?"

With a grin, Jordan stuck his tongue out and licked around the crown of Aaron's cock.

"Oh," Aaron moaned as Jordan worked him deeper into his throat, inch by inch. "You don't have to go all the way—fuck!" Aaron yelped as Jordan sucked and licked the length of the shaft. His own cock strained against the zipper of his pants, which he reached to release. But Aaron grabbed his hand before he could. "You're talented with your mouth. Bet your hips are just as good."

Jordan sucked hard as he slid Aaron from the embrace of his lips. He savored the drops of precome on his tongue and replied, "I think we should test that theory." He threw the rest of his uniform in the laundry basket and patted the bed next to him, where Aaron sat. Jordan had expected the other man to claim top position but was pleased they could skip that debate.

As Jordan opened the lube bottle, Aaron took it from him. "Let me," he whispered.

"Oh..." A moan interrupted Jordan as Aaron stroked the lube from the tip to the base. "What's the easiest way for you to bottom?" Jordan asked once he caught his breath.

"Either my back or my knees. Your pick."

Jordan stretched out on his side and wrapped his arms around Aaron when he joined him. "Ready to fly, Angel?"

"Please," he breathed, rolling onto his back. Jordan knelt between Aaron's long legs and brought his knees to his chest.

Adding extra lube to help accommodate his girth, Jordan pushed in slowly. They both sighed as he bottomed out. The two of them created a steady rhythm. Any thoughts were drowned out by cries of ecstasy. Jordan held back until the throbbing in his member became painful, at which point he stroked Aaron to release. The two men lay next to each other in silence, sticky and sated as their pulses evened. Jordan wondered if Aaron would leave right away. His question was answered when Aaron placed his head on his chest. Smiling down at him, Jordan murmured, "Beautiful."

"Not the word most people would use to describe me," Aaron responded.

"Then they must be blind. That isn't what I'm talking about though. Look down. The contrast between light and dark...it's a gorgeous combination," Jordan explained.

Aaron leaned up and kissed him. "You're a sap."

Chapter Six

AUGUST 2013, KABUL, AFGHANISTAN

Jordan arrived at the American embassy fifteen minutes early. The dream from the night before and making extra time to talk to Aaron this morning had vastly improved his mood. He greeted the MPs guarding the embassy, showed his ID, and made his way to the conference room to wait.

Colonel Bryant strode into the room and shook Jordan's hand. "Wonderful to see you, Captain!"

"Same to you, sir. You're looking well," Jordan lied. The lieutenant colonel had packed on quite a few pounds, making his belly as big as his voice.

"Thank you. The wife and I have taken up yoga, gentler on the joints." Bryant motioned to the chairs around the table. "Please take a seat. I'm sure you've been keeping up with the POW situation."

"As much as I can with the limited information I've been given."

"You have to understand we're limited in what we're able to share," Bryant began.

Jordan nodded, more to move the conversation along than agreeing with what the lieutenant colonel said. He had no interest in repeating the debate about who should receive privileged information. "Last I heard, the Afghanistan government had twenty of our soldiers. Do we have any report on their condition?"

"Unfortunately, five of those soldiers have been executed." Bryant slid a file folder across the table. "That is everything we know about the case. Be warned, the photographs of the executions are quite graphic."

Jordan flipped the folder open and scanned the pages. The photographs Bryant warned him about depicted four men and one woman, all of whom were hanged, shot, or decapitated. "That's unacceptable. What are our plans for recovery of the rest?" He struggled to exert control over the forcefulness of his voice.

"Of course, it's unacceptable, Captain. We're surrounded by savages!" Bryant released a breath and added, "The president believes that you are our best hope to bring our men and women home safely."

"What are their demands for the return of our soldiers?"

Colonel Bryant adjusted his tie before responding, "They want the US government to set an Islamic leader free. Problem is, we don't have him."

Jordan focused in on the words in front of him. Mehrdad Jalalabad, a high Muslim official, had disappeared during an American raid six months ago. "Are you sure?"

"I haven't even heard of him. I think the Afghan government is making the whole thing up as an excuse to kidnap and torture our soldiers," the LTC answered.

"If that were the case, it would make more sense to kill them on sight. Or torture and kill them after getting information. Not house them for months on end," Jordan told him. "I'm not questioning your knowledge, sir. I'm asking if perhaps someone else might know who he is or where he's being held."

"Don't you think I checked all the available resources? Our CIA expert came to the same conclusions I did," Colonel Bryant said.

Jordan snapped his gaze to meet with Bryant's. "You involved Aaron?"

"No, the one who's here, Foster."

Is not an expert. Jordan nodded again. Foster reminded Jordan of a puppy. Eager to learn and for approval, but Jordan needed a puppy like he needed a hole in the head...which was scarily possible in this situation.

"He'll accompany you to the meeting with Loya Jirga in six weeks' time," Bryant continued.

Afghanistan high council must require a sacrificial lamb. "Then, why isn't he here?"

"There will be plenty of time for collaboration, Captain."

Closing the file, Jordan asked, "If we don't have Jalalabad, what other options are available for freeing our soldiers? Has the Loya Jirga offered any alternatives?"

"No, that's all they claim to want."

Bryant shuffled papers on his side of the table. Jordan stared at him. "What would you like me to do?"

"Get the Americans out at any cost," Colonel Bryant said and stood. "We have faith in you, Captain."

"Thank you, sir." Jordan shook his hand and left the room with the file. He obviously had his work cut out for him if he was going to earn that faith.

Chapter Seven

SEPTEMBER 2013, BETHESDA, MARYLAND

"Aaron! Let's go," his brother, Chris, called from downstairs the day of the AC/DC concert.

"Just a second," he yelled back. "I'm sorry, Jordan, I have to go." Aaron directed his apology toward the computer as he pulled on his clothes.

Jordan laughed. "That's okay. Long-distance cuddling after Skype sex is overrated."

Aaron smiled at him. "We needed that though."

"We did," Jordan agreed. "You look hot, by the way."

"Thanks," Aaron answered, facing the mirror to spike his hair and evaluate his appearance. Tight jeans, black band shirt, and a touch of eyeliner. Not perfect, but it would do.

"No... I mean your face is flushed and sweaty. You look like you just finished working out." Jordan laughed again at Aaron's scowl.

"And whose fault is that?" Aaron threw back, though the teasing was worth it to hear Jordan laugh. It had become so rare lately. "Hey, fifty-one days."

"Can't wait," Jordan replied. "Have fun and call me when you get home, please."

"Are you sure? I don't want to wake you."

"I probably won't sleep. Worst case, I call you back."

Chris stomped up the stairs. "Aaron, we're going to be late! Let's go."

"Hi, Chris," Jordan called.

"Hey, Jay. Did I interrupt something?" Chris asked, standing in the doorway.

"No," Jordan said.

"Yes, you did," Aaron corrected.

"Sorry, but I don't want to be—"

"Late, yes, I know." Aaron rolled his eyes. "Love you, Jor."

"Love you too. I'll talk to you soon. Bye, Chris." Jordan chuckled as he ended the call.

Aaron grabbed his jacket and shut the laptop. "You were an hour late for your wedding, thirty minutes late for the birth of your daughter, and lost three jobs for constant tardiness. And yet, you're stressing about being late for a concert that doesn't start for three hours?" he demanded of Chris.

Chris shrugged. "At least I was on time for your wedding."

"Because I brought you," Aaron clarified, leading the way down the steps. "Where are we eating?"

"New place by the venue. I'll drive," Chris told him as they left the house.

"In your two-seat sports car? I think not." Aaron locked the door twice and motioned to his Hyundai SUV, where Chris joined him after a minute.

After settling in, Chris asked, "So, how's Jordan doing?"

"Hanging in there," Aaron replied as he started the car.

"What's that mean?"

Aaron grimaced. "I don't have the details. This deployment seems different for him." Rather, he didn't have any *new* details. All he knew was that Jordan was tenser than usual. "Annie like her new job?"

"You're changing the subject."

"It's polite to go along with people who do that," Aaron countered. "Tell me what's new with your wife and daughter."

Chris detailed his wife's pharmaceutical job and his little girl's adjustment to daycare while Aaron's mind wandered. The story never changed. Annie hated every job she ever had. Chris worked sporadically and always had a get-rich-quick scheme ready to launch, but had had to ask Aaron for rent money more than once.

"Are you listening?" Chris asked.

"Sorry, I zoned out for a second. What was the last thing you said?"

"That I think this business might work out. Dad agrees."

"You got Dad involved?" *Again.* Aaron groaned.

"He thinks it's going to be profitable. You should be more supportive."

Aaron might have answered had they not pulled up to the venue lot, but, then again, probably not. Nothing he said made a difference. "How close is the restaurant?" he asked.

"Couple doors down," Chis answered. "You can park here."

Inevitably, the hot place a few doors down from the venue overflowed with concertgoers. So Aaron and Chris made their way to a sports bar two blocks away. Aaron flitted his gaze over the menu on the wall and ordered a beer and fries.

"That's all you're having?" Chris questioned.

"They don't serve salads here," Troy cut in from the other side of Aaron. "He doesn't eat meat he hasn't cooked himself."

"Not true," Aaron protested. "I don't eat meat cooked by people I don't know. Big difference."

Troy held out his hand to Chris. "Hi, I'm Troy. Aaron and I work together."

"I'm Chris, his brother. Are you alone?"

Pointing behind him, Troy replied, "No, I'm here with my friend. We're eating and then going to the concert."

"Hey, so are we. Why don't you join us?" Chris wore a goofy grin as he made the invitation.

"Love to," Troy said and went to his table.

"I didn't know you had friends." Two beers and already Chris thought he was funny.

Gonna be a long night. "He's a coworker, actually a superior," Aaron explained. *That my husband doesn't like.* Aaron had not gone out of his way to avoid Troy over the past few weeks, per se, but he was also busy during lunches. So, the two of them had not gotten any alone time.

"Sorry," Chris said, and Aaron shrugged.

Troy walked back over with a woman whose breasts were the largest part of her body. He introduced her as Laura. After greeting both of them, Laura gravitated to Chris, who automatically cleared the counter for her and offered the seat next to him.

"He's married," Aaron told Troy.

"Never stopped her before." Aaron glared at him, and Troy added, "Would you relax? They're both adults."

Aaron laughed. "Someone ought to give Chris that memo."

"You the protective big brother?" Troy asked.

Aaron took a swig of his beer. "He's my older brother. Not that you'd know it by talking to him."

Troy nodded. "Thought you weren't coming to the concert."

"Never said that. I said I wasn't as much of an AC/DC fan as my brother." Aaron passed Troy the fry basket. "Want some?"

"Thanks," he answered and picked at a fry. "You all right?"

Noting the time, Aaron said, "Yeah, sure. We better leave."

Placing a hand on Aaron's arm, Troy questioned, "What's wrong?"

"Troy." Aaron took a deep breath. "You're above me at work. I'm not sure it's appropriate for me to open up to you."

"So, work is stressing you out?"

Aaron shook his head.

"Then, I don't see any reason we can't be friends outside of the agency." At Aaron's hesitancy, Troy added, "I can sign a nondisclosure agreement if that would make you feel better."

"No. I..." Their work relationship was Aaron's best justification. "I'm not worried about that."

Another long silence passed before Troy implored, "Come on, I know how lonely the distance of deployment can be, especially for someone who's not a part of the military community."

"How do you know that?" Aaron questioned, finishing his beer.

"Your ID is on the bar," Troy explained. "I'd recognize an on-base address."

Aaron paid for his tab. "Jordan's an officer. He took the housing allowance and used it for a townhouse."

"Many officers choose that route. Nothing wrong with it, but it's more difficult for their spouses to form connections among people who would understand them best," Troy told him.

"That's where you're wrong. Military spouses aren't all the same. The bases cater to heterosexual families with kids," Aaron pointed out, tucking away his license. "I've connected with a few gay spouses, but it's only been recently that the option was open. All of which you know."

"Yes, I do. The organization is changing, albeit slowly." Troy released a breath. "When I enlisted, you could be imprisoned if someone so much as suspected you of same-sex preferences. Never mind Don't Ask, Don't Tell. The closet had a damn steel door with a deadlock."

Aaron gave him a sideways glance. "Is that why you married a woman?"

"If you asked me then, I would have sworn up and down that I loved her. Maybe I did, but I could never force myself to be attracted to her," Troy said. "It was worth it though. I never would have had my daughter without her." He leaned closer to Aaron, who countered by resting on his elbows further back. "I'm not going to hurt you."

"I know." *I wouldn't allow it.*

Troy smirked, as though pleased with himself for a reason Aaron couldn't name. "So what's on your mind?"

"Nothing specific. Collection of everything. Jordan is more stressed than I have ever seen him, and Chris is set to bankrupt my parents any day now." Aaron told Troy a little about Chris's latest scheme.

After studying Aaron for a long moment, Troy said, "I don't think Chris's situation is really concerning you. I think you added that to mask your worry about Jordan. What's going on there?"

Aaron licked his lips and took his turn to evaluate the other man. His eyes showed interest. And hey, maybe Troy could help. *But Jordan doesn't like him,* he argued with himself. *But just as a leader. Jordan could only know Troy from a distance. People's policies don't necessarily match their personalities.* He relaxed his posture and said, "You would know more about that than I would. I was taken off the case a couple of weeks ago. I think the mission intensified or something."

"What if… Jordan wasn't ready to quit, and that's why he seems more distant than other deployments? He could be regretting his rash decision," Troy tried.

"No, if that were the case, I would know. Jordan and I share an intense connection and have since the day we met," Aaron told him.

"All right. I can tell you that every mission is different. Maybe the work is more involved this time. I've had missions where we sat around in our barracks for months on end and missions where we were constantly solving a problem."

Aaron shook his head and stood up straight again. *Guess Troy won't be able to help after all.* "Yeah, Troy, we've been together over eleven years. I understand the variance of assignments. I've been there. It's his disposition that's different. Everything else can be explained by changing work." He glanced to his right. "Where are Chris and Laura?"

Troy glanced at his phone and showed Aaron Laura's text message.

Didn't want to disturb your cozy conversation. Meet you at the corner after the show in case we're lost in the crowd.

"Great," Aaron muttered, patting his pockets for his keys, wallet, and cell phone. If she described their conversation as cozy, what did everyone else in the bar think? He rushed out.

"Hey!" Troy ran to catch up to him. "I'm sorry. I didn't mean to dismiss you."

"Don't worry about it. Everyone else does." Aaron eyed him over his shoulder, not slowing his stride.

"I'm not everyone else," Troy insisted, gasping for breath.

"The platitudes you offered suggest otherwise. Seriously, it's not a big deal. You and I are fine. Let's rock out." Aaron considered feeling badly for outpacing Troy so easily, but sometimes it was best to use natural advantages.

Troy made it to his side when they had to wait for a walk signal. "What do you want from me?"

"Nothing," Aaron answered. "I'm perfectly happy with my life the way it is."

"I don't believe that."

Fucking longest light ever. "You don't have to." He whipped toward him. "All I ask is for people to listen to me. You asked me what was wrong; I told you. I don't expect you to do anything." Troy leaned on the light pole, panting. Aaron blinked at him. "Are you okay?"

"Yes. I have asthma." Troy gulped in air as he spoke. "I can't run as well as I used to."

Aaron led him to a bench and eased him down. "Do you need an inhaler?"

"No, please give me a minute," Troy responded.

Once Troy's breathing returned to normal, Aaron pressed, "Why did you run if it triggers an asthma attack?"

"I had to catch up with you."

"Why?"

Raising his gaze to meet Aaron's, Troy said, "Because I find you interesting, and I don't think it would hurt either one of us to have an extra friend."

Troy's voice was sincere enough that Aaron didn't question his statement. Not to say he understood it, but no harm in a second chance, right? Aaron was probably oversensitive anyway. Aaron dismissed the nagging in his gut to his oversensitivity. "When did you get turned on to AC/DC?"

JORDAN SNATCHED HIS phone from the side table as Aaron's ring tone sounded. "Hey, Angel, how was the show?"

"Decent," Aaron answered. "You're much more awake than you should be at 7:00 a.m. on a Saturday."

"I've been up since five, working out with the troops." Jordan leaned down on the bed. "Tell me about the show. What's new with Chris?"

"Chris is...Chris," Aaron said. "I'm putting you on speaker while I get changed."

"Thanks for the heads-up." Jordan covered a yawn with his hand. "Did Chris come home with you?"

"He, uh, found someone else to stay with tonight," Aaron responded from a few feet away.

"Someone like his wife?"

"Mm, no, this woman had very little in common with his wife." The disgust was clear in Aaron's statement.

"Wow, did he bring her with him or meet her there?" Jordan asked, raising his voice over the rustling of covers.

"Neither." Aaron brought the phone to his ear. "She was at the bar beforehand with..." He paused for three beats before continuing, "Troy."

"Troy...Hart?" Jordan questioned.

"Yes."

"Did you plan to meet him?" Jordan coached his tone to remain curious.

"No, he happened to be there, so we all hung out," Aaron answered carefully.

Jordan exhaled, silently berating himself for making Aaron feel like he had to hesitate. His issues with Hart shouldn't affect his husband, especially not from across the world. "Cool, did you have fun?"

"Eventually." Aaron laughed a little, demonstrating his relief. "It was awkward at first because of the work shit."

"Work shit? What do you mean?"

"He's higher on the food chain than I am. So it took me a bit to relax," Aaron explained. "But Chris asked him to join us after he came to say hello. Would have been even more awkward to uninvite him."

Rolling onto his side for comfort, Jordan said, "Makes sense. So, what's he like?" *When he isn't making precarious decisions.*

"Eh, he's fine, I guess. He's desperate for people to like him. You know how I feel about that," Aaron replied.

Jordan did. Aaron had even less patience for fake people than Jordan did, which left very little room.

"Jordan, would it bother you if I were friends with him? Please tell me if it would."

Yes, Jordan thought, but that was not the correct response. Well, it might be if he could offer details as to why, but he couldn't, so he had to give the acceptable answer. "No. He's not my favorite person, but that has nothing to do with you. Hang out with him if you enjoy his company."

"I kind of feel bad for him. He's all right though," Aaron concluded. "Oh, the concert—the band did two encores, including the longest version of 'Highway to Hell' I've ever heard."

"Did they put the guitar solo in the middle or the end?" Jordan asked.

"Middle. Hold on." Aaron sent the video through text message.

"Thanks," Jordan said. "Are you tired?"

"I don't mind staying awake to talk to you."

"That would be a yes. You don't have to stay up. We'll talk in twelve hours. And now that it's after midnight your time, I will see you in fifty days. I love you."

"I love you too," Aaron replied sleepily. "Talk soon."

As they ended their call, Jordan flopped onto his back and rubbed his face. He trusted Aaron completely, but never Hart. He fisted the sheets as the memory of exactly why flooded his mind.

Chapter Eight

ONE YEAR EARLIER, KABUL, AFGHANISTAN

"The major general wants me to order my soldiers to do...what?" Jordan asked. In another month, his deployment would be over. And in two months, he would be up for a below-the-line promotion from captain to major. All he had to do was keep his head down and not make any catastrophic decisions.

"Promote the United States' image to Afghan civilians. The same as always, *Captain*," Colonel Bryant replied, with an emphasis on Jordan's title.

Yes, I know I'm below you and him. "Of course, sir, but we have not had prior success in the area he's asking them to infiltrate. It's one of the few localities where Taliban support remains strong."

Bryant's eyes flashed with doubt before he turned away from Jordan and made his way to the window across the room. "General Hart believes we need to focus on changing their opinion."

Jordan stared at his superior. "Have you shown him the data about the unlikeliness of conversion?"

"He has the reports, but as I'm sure you're aware, part of the reason the US and NATO have been unsuccessful in altering public opinion is the disproportionate percentage of civilian deaths in the region," the lieutenant colonel said. "You are to order the men and women in your platoon to bring children's books, medical supplies, food, water, and blankets to the homeless. We are striving to show the citizens that the United States has their best interests at heart. It is vital for them to know they're cared for."

"Sir," Jordan started as he strode toward Bryant. "We have tried peace maneuvers several times in that locality."

Colonel Bryant faced Jordan again, his hands clenched together behind his back. "Yes, Captain, we've lost hundreds of men and women. I am fully aware of the danger." He worked the tension from his body with measured breaths before continuing. "However, General Hart has many years of experience and feels with extra security measures we can help those in need."

"Have you personally explained that all the security measures in the world won't advance our agenda or their well-being if we cannot access the civilians? Our last intel report indicated they may be guarded by an extremist group."

The lieutenant colonel wore a path into the carpet as his forehead moistened. "I shared that information. I also told him about the distrust of Westerners."

"What was his response?" Jordan questioned.

After a moment of silence, Colonel Bryant stopped and met Jordan's gaze. "He added more money to the aid we'll offer."

"So, he didn't listen to a word you said."

The lieutenant colonel shrugged. "General Hart has engaged the support of international relief organizations for the aid of the impoverished Afghan people. The president has praised the idea." He shook his head. "The orders are in place. It's out of our hands. We will take every precaution for the soldiers. You will tell them at a meeting tonight, and the mission begins on Thursday at 0900 hours."

Jordan nodded, resigned. "Yes, sir. I will assist them in any way that I can."

"By ensuring that every single member has a clear understanding of the plan and meeting me here once they have left to keep in constant communication with First Lieutenant Jackson," Colonel Bryant told Jordan, all doubt removed from his voice.

"Jackson is not ready for that level of leadership."

"You have trained him well, and with mission-specific preparation, I am sure he will rise to the occasion," Bryant countered. "I need you here."

Alive. You need me alive. "I don't abandon my people."

"I told you that the members of your platoon will be well-protected and prepared. However, I cannot allow one of my best leaders to take chances with his life. Difficult decisions must be made. Once again, your orders are to meet with the members of your platoon tonight and prepare them for their mission at 0900 hours on Thursday. By 0915, you are to report here to guide First Lieutenant Jackson through any problems that should arise." Colonel Bryant held Jordan's gaze long enough to remind him of his place.

Jordan opened his mouth to accept the lieutenant colonel's orders, because that was what he'd spent years training to do. But he stopped himself. He was more than his training, and damn more than his place. "No. If you insist on following through with this mission, then I am going to stand with my platoon."

His superior inclined his head. "Captain Collins, I did not ask a question."

"Neither did I. I will not send my people on a suicide mission alone."

"They will be—"

"Protected? Prepared?" Jordan interrupted, his tone no longer neutral. "That's bullshit, and you know it. General Hart is wrong." He paused to consider. "Then again, maybe he's right. Maybe he intends to have our troops killed to garner sympathy for the war effort in the US. Maybe this isn't about winning our enemies over at all. I think it's about improving our ratings back home." The two men locked gazes for another moment that felt like an hour before Jordan concluded, "I refuse to order the men and women who answer to me to unnecessarily enter a situation they are not trained to deal with."

Colonel Bryant nodded. "While I admire your devotion to your charges, the mission has been ordered from beyond either of our levels of influence. So, Captain Collins, I am telling you one more time to carry out your orders."

"No, sir, I will not endanger the people who trust me without due cause."

"I understand, Captain." The lieutenant colonel turned away again, but Jordan felt no relief at his words. "Effective immediately, you no longer have a platoon to manage on this mission. We will have you on the first plane home tomorrow. Dismissed."

His mind reeled. Dismissed from...what? His post, yes, but...was there more? How much trouble was he in? After realizing Colonel Bryant would say nothing else to him, Jordan left the room.

ON THURSDAY AT 0900 Afghanistan time, 2:00 a.m. EST, Jordan removed his duffel bag from the overhead compartment and slung it over his shoulder. Never in his life had he felt like such a complete and utter failure as when the stewardess paid him extra attention and the pilot came out to thank him. *For what?* Jordan wanted to scream. *My one goal in my job is to keep people safe. I couldn't do that.*

After a short wait in the customs line, Jordan made his way to the baggage claim where his father, Elliot, wrapped him in a hug. "Welcome home, son."

"Thank you." Jordan pulled away to retrieve his suitcase from the belt.

"Let me help," his dad offered.

"I can—"

"I know," Elliot interrupted. "But the bag on your shoulder is heavy enough."

Since there was no point in arguing, Jordan nodded and followed him out to the car.

"I'm sorry to have asked you to pick me up so late," Jordan said when they were settled.

His father rolled his eyes at him. "I will not insult either of us by properly responding to that, but I did wonder if I was taking you to your house or mine."

"My house, please."

"Then..."

"I didn't know what to say to Aaron. If I just show up, I might convince him not to ask questions," Jordan explained.

"Or he could mistake you for an intruder and shoot you."

Jordan laughed for the first time in days. "I'll make my identity clear."

A moment passed before Elliot hedged, "I assume you're in trouble?"

"I assume I am." Jordan met his eyes. "I'm not double-talking you. I really don't know. I was dismissed from my post in Afghanistan, but my CO told me nothing else."

"Why? Can you tell me? I understand if you can't."

Jordan inhaled. His dad understood because he'd served for thirty-five years. "I refused to run a mission sanctioned by General Hart." At his father's silence, he added, "I couldn't, Dad."

"Sometimes, Jordan, you have to put yourself in harm's way for the greater good. I'm sure you would have known enough to be safe." Elliot stopped when Jordan shook his head.

"I would have been safe. The LTC had me with him. My platoon members are not safe. I could not give the order," Jordan asserted. "Maybe I should have followed the script and done as I was told, but I couldn't."

"All right," Elliot said as he pulled up in front of Jordan and Aaron's house. "I trust you. I'm sure you made the best decision you were able to, given the circumstances. Let me know if I can do anything to help with the discipline board."

"Thank you."

"Of course, son." Elliot leaned over and hugged him across the seats. "Call me tomorrow."

Jordan agreed and grabbed his two bags from the back seat. On the trudge up to his dark front door, he rethought his decision to not give Aaron a warning of his return. *Too late to do anything about it now.* He used the glow of his cell phone to unlock the door and waved to his dad as he stepped inside. He turned on the living room light and dropped his bags.

"Jordan?" Aaron called from the top of the steps. "Is that you?"

"How did you know?" Jordan embraced his husband when Aaron flew down the stairs into his arms. He sniffed hard into Aaron's chest.

Aaron rubbed his back under his uniform shirt. "LTC talked to Keller."

"What did he say?" Jordan asked, turning his cheek to one side and looking up at Aaron.

"That some blowhard major general is pissing around with lives, and you weren't playing."

"Pretty much," Jordan replied. The CIA had called Aaron home a week ago and given him a different assignment, which must have made sense to someone on some level, but neither Jordan nor Aaron understood. "I couldn't."

"I know, love." Aaron simply pressed a kiss to Jordan's lips and said, "Come to bed. We'll figure it out in the morning."

"I can't sleep. It is morning for me," Jordan told him. "You should though. You have work in a few hours."

"You know what? I haven't taken any vacation days this year. I think I should do that, don't you?"

Jordan tightened his hold on him and inhaled his sweet scent. "Balance is important." He stretched up for another kiss, which Aaron gifted him. "Angel, I need you," Jordan breathed.

"I'm right here," Aaron promised.

As though reading Jordan's need for skin-to-skin contact, Aaron stepped back and stripped. Jordan followed his example. They left a trail of clothing on the way to their room. Jordan tugged Aaron toward him, melding their naked bodies together. "You're so warm, Angel. So warm," he murmured, kissing his chest.

Aaron tilted Jordan's chin up and their mouths met, tongues lingering, exploring the soft caverns they knew so well. "I am so glad to have you home," he whispered, guiding him toward the bed. "You are brave and strong."

Jordan opened his eyes. "You don't have all the details."

"No, but I know you, and that means the details don't matter, at least not for my statement to be true." Aaron nudged Jordan onto the bed.

Missing the contact, Jordan pulled Aaron down between his legs and wrapped his arms around him. He squeezed his eyes shut as he stroked his hands down Aaron's body. At some indistinguishable point, Jordan began physically reacting to Aaron's caresses and kisses. Aaron sat up with a satisfied smile and dug through the nightstand drawer. He extended the lube to Jordan, who pushed it back to him. A flash of worry washed over Jordan. But Aaron kissed it away. So Jordan spread his legs further apart to expose his vulnerability to the one person he trusted to take care of it.

Their eyes locked while Aaron lubed them both and breached Jordan's entrance. "Relax for me, baby," Aaron crooned into Jordan's ear. The words widened Jordan's channel enough to embrace Aaron's member. The two men moved rhythmically, keeping as much skin-to-skin contact as possible until their breaths hitched in quiet announcement of shared release. "My hero," Aaron whispered.

Those words, spoken with the true genuineness, destroyed Jordan's wall of control. Jordan had no idea how long sweat, semen, and tears seared him to Aaron's shoulder that night, but he eventually fell into an exhausted slumber.

BY THE NEXT morning, Aaron had cleaned Jordan of their shared fluids. They spent the following two days talking and connecting. Aaron offered quiet support while Jordan awaited news of his punishment and the result of the mission.

"Aren't there more reliable sources of information?" Aaron asked on Friday morning while Jordan flipped between news stations on the television.

"I can't guarantee they'll tell me anything," Jordan answered, not taking his eyes off the screen. "Besides, I don't need to hear the reporters' analysis. All I need to know is how many people died."

Aaron sat next to him and kissed his hand. "Can you contact someone on the mission?"

"They're incommunicado for another three days," Jordan told him.

"Then isn't that when the media would hear?" Aaron took the remote from Jordan. Before he could protest, Aaron said, "I love you more than anything, but I will not tolerate Fox News."

Jordan smiled. "Actually, their military reporting is pretty acc..." He grabbed the remote back, turning the volume up as the words "Relief Mission Stalled in Afghanistan" appeared across the screen. *Stalled?*

"Due to an unprecedented refusal to carry out orders, Platoon 82 of the US Army denied homeless Afghanistan citizens needed supplies," the reporter droned.

"According to army sources, the mission was stalled until new leadership could be found, since the platoon captain was sent back to the United States," her coworker added.

"Yes!" Jordan screamed and kissed Aaron on the lips.

Aaron hugged him tight. "I'm so proud of you."

"And if I'm separated from service?" Jordan asked.

"Then I'll know it was for a good reason, and I'll be all the more proud."

THE MILITARY DISCIPLINE board denied him early promotion but took no other action against him.

Chapter Nine

SEPTEMBER 2013, KABUL, AFGHANISTAN

"Hey, Angel, thanks for the package," Jordan said as he started their Skype call the night before his first negotiation meeting with the captors of the American POWs. "I can't tell you how much I missed Butterfingers."

Aaron laughed. "I'm glad you got it. I was afraid whoever goes through the soldiers' mail would miss chocolate too."

"Yeah, I'm sure she does, but the staff sergeant in charge knows better than to steal an officer's candy." Jordan began disassembling his uniform as they spoke.

"Oh, I bet she could find some reason to label it against regulations." Aaron stretched his arms above his head. "How was your day?"

"Let's just say the Butterfingers and T-shirts helped immensely." Jordan slipped one on. Aaron had bought shirts in Jordan's size, slept in them, and mailed them in an air-sealed bag, so they still smelled like him when they arrived.

"Did you see the pictures I included?" Aaron asked.

Jordan tried not to cringe in fear that Aaron had sent inappropriate pictures. *Those* the staff sergeant would take. Instead, he found a few shots of Aaron posing in the shirts, which—because they fit Jordan—were at the same time too big and too short. So they made for commendable belly-dancing costumes. Or that's what Jordan assumed Aaron was doing.

"Oh, God, you win," Jordan told him through fits of laughter.

"I will be very upset if I find out that you passed those pictures around to the other officers or platoon members." Aaron injected mock-sternness into his voice.

"Well, no, don't want to make them jealous."

"Exactly. This—" Aaron swept his hand over his body. "—is yours and yours alone."

"Glad to hear that." Jordan sat on his bed again. "Anything new at home?"

"Yes, actually, the fridge broke."

"Like, completely broke, or needs to be looked at?"

"Repairman came yesterday. It'll cost less money to replace than fix," Aaron explained.

Jordan chewed his lower lip. "Do we have enough in the joint account to pay for it?" The majority of their money went into their shared account, but they each kept one paycheck a month in their own accounts for personal expenses.

"We do, but the mortgage is going to be tight," Aaron answered. "Sorry, I don't want to stress you out."

"You're fine. All right, I'll transfer last week's paycheck in."

"I can put it on credit," Aaron offered, but Jordan shook his head.

"You know I don't like using credit."

"Well, I like you being able to eat. The store has a plan available with no interest for the first six months."

Jordan released a breath. "I would eat fine, even with the loss of one paycheck, but the payment plan works as long as we meet the six-month deadline."

"Babe," Aaron said, drawing Jordan's eyes to the screen. "Thirty-six days."

"Then what?"

"Then we can talk about money and refrigerators in person," he responded, eliciting another chuckle from Jordan. "No, in thirty-six days, I will be waiting at the airport with my arms open."

"Mm, I'll run into them and give you a hard kiss—"

"Which will make certain other body parts hard. Some people will clap, some will take pictures, but nothing they do will affect us. Because we'll be together, so the rest of the world will fade away. Like it always does."

Jordan lifted his shoulder to catch Aaron's scent and enhance the visualization.

"They'd really clap if they could follow us home," Aaron said.

"Yes, they would. Thank you. That was exactly what I needed tonight."

"You're welcome."

"I may be out of touch for a few days," Jordan said, though it made his heart ache.

"Please get in contact when you can, even if it's only a text or an email to let me know you're all right." Aaron barely hid his concern.

"Of course, Angel. I love you."

"I love you too. Be safe. Please," Aaron directed.

"Always. I'll talk to you soon," Jordan promised, and they exchanged good nights before ending their Skype call.

With a heavy heart, Jordan turned off the light and begged for sleep he didn't expect to come.

Chapter Ten

SEPTEMBER 2013, KABUL, AFGHANISTAN

Jordan went over the plan in his head on the way to the Afghan prison in a bulletproof, tinted-window Hummer surrounded by military security. He and another officer, First Lieutenant Doug Parks, would offer members of the Loya Jirga, the Afghanistan grand council, up to four hundred million dollars to release the American prisoners—assuming they proved the soldiers were still alive. Since Colonel Bryant told him about the POWs, Jordan had been in contact with prison officials who sent daily photographic proof. Today, Jordan would take the pictures for his superiors. The Hummer jarred to a stop for the driver to show identification at the prison gate for admittance. They parked in front of the administration building a few feet from the gate. Jordan's senses were on high alert as he left the Hummer with security on all sides. He noted the physical details of the stone-faced guards at the entrance.

Inside the building, the uniformed group strode down a long hall with chipping white paint and pictures of Afghan leaders on the walls. Upon arrival at the conference room, Jordan took his place next to Parks. "Good morning, Lieutenant."

"Morning, sir," Parks replied. One of his brightest men, Parks was Jordan's first choice to accompany him today, and the one he would recommend to take his place at the end of his commission. Jordan was grateful that Foster had called in sick and would spend the day in bed, instead of joining them here.

They would have continued their conversation, but the door opened, admitting two members of the Loya Jirga, Abdul Obaid and Anwar Nadar. The four men exchanged greetings and stiff pleasantries.

"I am told you are not in need of an English translator. Is this correct?" Nadar questioned them in Farsi.

"Yes, it is," Jordan answered in the man's native tongue.

"Are you sure? We would not want to confuse you," Nadar jeered.

"Language will not be a problem," Jordan reiterated. "Before anything is discussed, we would like to be taken to see the Americans."

"As I understand it, you have Americans all around you, or do the light camouflage uniforms deceive me?" Obaid questioned.

"The POWs," Parks clarified. "We will talk after we ensure their well-being."

"Were the pictures not enough?" Nadar pressed.

"No. We discussed this on the phone, Nadar," Jordan told him. "Take us to them."

The two groups made their way to the next building. The temperature in the prison elevated twenty degrees from the outside. The heat saturated the air with a combination of body odor and decay. "Is there no air-conditioning?" Jordan asked.

"We do what we can," Obaid answered. "These are criminals, after all, Captain. Perhaps, your convicts would be repentant if they weren't made so comfortable in prisons."

Jordan could have pointed out rampant human rights violations in the prison around him, but instead took photographs and notes on a sheet of paper. A woman sat behind a desk wearing a hijab along with linen pants and top. He had never seen one without a burka on in Afghanistan. While no longer required by law, most still wore them regularly. This woman, however, was different. She met Jordan's eyes for a full ten seconds.

"That is my wife, Captain Collins. I suggest you look away," Nadar ordered.

"I am no threat to your wife." All the same, Jordan averted his gaze from the brazen woman. "Where are the American prisoners?"

Nadar twitched and stared Jordan down, as though issuing a warning. "Follow me," he said, pressing a button to open the steel doors.

The Afghan prisoners called out from either side of them, some for help, others jeering and spitting as they passed through the cell blocks. Around another corner stood four cells, three of which held four Americans. The last held three.

"You may address them only in Farsi," Obaid told Jordan and Parks.

Jordan and Parks spoke to the imprisoned soldiers—who appeared to be better-treated than their Afghan counterparts—through their cell bars. Parks promised them that they were there to bring them home.

After the discussion, Nadar and Obaid led the Americans back to the conference room. "What are you after?" Parks asked the Afghanistan leaders.

"After? Your slang does not translate well, Lieutenant," Obaid told him.

Jordan surveyed the guards inside the room. One of his guards fidgeted far more than was allowed. He made a mental note to reprimand the soldier later. "How much money would you require to release the American POWs?"

"Money? Do you believe we would risk an escalation of the war effort for want of money?" Obaid spat.

No. But he couldn't say that. "Why, then?"

"You Americans never listen the first time you're told something," Nadar scoffed. "We've had the same demands for years. We want you out of our country and our people returned to their normal lives."

"So why did you risk escalation now?" Jordan pressed.

Nadar leaned forward. "Because you did, Captain. You have Mehrdad Jalalabad in Guantanamo Bay. If we don't get him back, more of your soldiers will die in our prison."

"We don't have him." *That I could find.* "Unless you can prove otherwise, I suggest you release our soldiers."

Obaid removed his thick glasses. The fidgeting from behind Jordan became more erratic. The air thickened. Jordan shot his hand down to the sidearm strapped to his thigh.

"Don't even think about it, Captain," Nadar hissed, one of his guards pointing a gun to Parks's head.

Within seconds, a steel grip held Jordan immobile against his chair and a sweet-smelling cloth covered his face. Two gunshots rang out, followed by blackness.

A NIGHTMARE WOKE Aaron up and set his pulse on fire. He clutched at Jordan's side of the bed. Cold. *No!*

Chapter Eleven

THREE YEARS AND NINE MONTHS EARLIER

Jordan kissed down the back of Aaron's neck. "Get up," he whispered excitedly.

"Keep kissing my neck and it won't be a problem." Aaron turned over but rolled onto his stomach when he caught sight of Jordan. "Oh, no, you're grinning. It's too early for grinning."

"You don't even know what time it is," Jordan protested.

"Will that knowledge change my opinion?"

The clock glared red digits reading 6:15. "No, but get up anyway. Please? I'll make it worth your while."

Aaron sighed and touched their lips together as he sat. "I can make it worth your while to stay in bed."

"Later. I promise to earn it," Jordan told him.

As Aaron shed the covers, he whined, "Why are we awake before 7:00 a.m. on a Saturday?"

"I will show you if you stop whining, take a shower, get dressed, and meet me downstairs." Aaron simply stood there staring for a moment, so Jordan added, "I love you."

"Mm, I love sleep but will accept coffee. Then I will love you." Aaron wrapped his arms around Jordan. "All right, I lied. I love you and your crazy self right now."

Jordan tilted his face up for a kiss. "I know, Angel. I waited as long as I could to wake you."

"Sure, you did," Aaron teased as he pulled away. "What should I wear?"

"Something warm."

"Will we be outside?"

Jordan grinned again and walked out the bedroom door. "We're going to fly." They had been training for months to skydive. Rather, Aaron had had to train; Jordan had learned with the army many years ago. Now that Jordan was a certified instructor, they'd be able to do a tandem jump without anyone else involved. Jordan set a hot mug of coffee next to Aaron's plate, and a newspaper on the other side. He went into the kitchen and poured the blueberry pancake batter on the griddle. His father texted to confirm Jordan and Aaron's planned landing spot. The next message read: *R U sure?*

Yes, Jordan typed back. *It isn't my first time skydiving. We'll be fine. See you on the ground.*

Elliot was not asking about the jump, and Jordan knew it. But the only person who could make him doubt what he had planned was Aaron, who circled his waist from behind and kissed his cheek.

"Good news in the paper today," Aaron murmured into Jordan's ear.

Jordan kissed his lips. "I thought so. We have pancakes and bacon for breakfast. Hungry?"

"Very, thanks," Aaron answered, all the grumpiness gone. He took the bacon out of the microwave as Jordan plated the pancakes. "Should we have a big breakfast if we're jumping?"

"We have to drive a bit," Jordan replied, sitting across from Aaron.

"How far's a bit?"

"Seven hours. Hope you don't have a date tonight."

Aaron tilted his head back. "We're going jumping seven hours away?"

"Yes, and to answer your next question, because it's romantic."

"Fair enough," Aaron said. "About this newspaper article..."

"When we get there." Jordan smiled to himself and bit a piece of bacon.

"So, let me get this straight. You decided where we are going, what we are doing, when we got there, and now you're dictating when we will have conversations?" Aaron cocked an eyebrow at him when Jordan gave him a nod. "What do I get to decide?"

Meeting his eyes, Jordan responded, "Your answer, but that'll probably depend on the phrasing of the question, so you'll have to wait."

Aaron cut up his pancake in silence. Jordan took a moment to gaze at the man across from him. The one who'd never cared about his military titles, education, or money. Aaron's quick wit had kept Jordan riveted from their very first night together. And today, Jordan would find out if they'd have forever.

"What time's the jump?" Aaron questioned.

"Four. We'll leave after breakfast." Jordan reached across the table and squeezed his hand. "Are you excited?"

"I am, though, maybe a bit nervous. Are you?"

Locking their gazes, Jordan answered, "Not about jumping."

Aaron kissed his hand and smiled. "Nothing else to be nervous about."

Jordan returned the smile. By the sparkle in Aaron's eyes, Jordan deduced that he knew what he planned to ask, and the answer. Not that he could take it for granted. "Ready to go?" He received silent agreement.

They cleaned up and Jordan grabbed their suitcase, since neither of them would want to drive seven hours there and seven hours back in one day. True to form, Aaron was a useless driving companion. Whenever he rode, he fell asleep with the turn of the ignition, leaving Jordan plenty of time to think, but Jordan had already envisioned the life he desired, and it had always included Aaron by his side. Now he had to convince Aaron of the same.

Once in the Niagara Falls hotel in upstate New York, Jordan pulled Aaron close and pressed their lips together. "I'm going to take care of you, Angel."

"You always do," he replied.

They held hands on the way to the lobby, and Jordan led him around a corner to avoid their gathered families and friends.

"Move faster! Your legs are longer than mine," Jordan reminded him.

Aaron ran ahead. "I was being nice. Let's see you catch up."

Doubling his sprint, Jordan pushed Aaron into the side of the plane. "I will always catch you," he said. Aaron wrapped his arms around Jordan and bent for a kiss.

Before their lips touched, the pilot stuck her head out. "Hey, Jordan, let's go," she called.

Jordan pecked Aaron and pulled away. "Dana, I'd like you to meet my boyfriend, Aaron. Aaron, Dana was the officer who decided our country was better served with me on the ground than flying planes."

Aaron laughed and shook her hand. "Thanks for that."

"No problem. I've been out of the army for a few years now," she explained.

That was why Jordan had known he could call her for help on what he deemed "his most important mission."

Dana had no more connection to the military. So she couldn't get him in trouble. "This is Aaron's first jump."

"But I've completed all the classes," Aaron assured her.

"Jordan wouldn't bring you if you hadn't," she responded. "Suit up, guys. Fifteen minutes until takeoff."

Jordan helped Aaron into his jumpsuit and breathed a sigh of relief that it fit. His height provided quite a few obstacles for clothing. Jumping gear was no different. After making sure Aaron was situated, he assembled his gear: jumpsuit, packed rig, and harness.

"Hey." Jordan placed his hand on Aaron's cheek and held it there until Aaron met his eyes. "The jump is going to be amazing. We both know what we're doing. Dana and I both checked the rig. Nothing will go wrong. I think once you make the jump, you'll find flying very natural."

"And why's that?" Aaron asked.

"Because all angels should fly," Jordan replied as he stepped onto the plane and shut the hatch door. "Ready when you are, Dana." She gave him the thumbs-up signal and radioed the control tower. "Angel, about that newspaper article," Jordan began, partly to assuage the mounting fear on Aaron's face.

"What?"

"Did you see the newspaper article next to your breakfast plate this morning?" Jordan asked.

"Murder in the metro?" Aaron tried, then amended, "DC approved same-sex marriage. It's great, but how is it relevant to us?"

"I think our marriage would be sort of like sky-diving," Jordan speculated. At Aaron's confusion, Jordan explained, "Angel... I help you fly, push you to do new things, feel deeper, believe in things you wouldn't consider. And you always bring me back to Earth. You've taught me the allure of the comfortable. I am so, so lucky to be the man you let behind your walls. Will you make it forever?"

Aaron kissed him hard. "I love you, and nothing would make me happier than to marry you, but the military..."

"Has nothing to do with our commitment to each other. I truly believe that someday even the military will join the modern era. And if not? I get out at the end of my commission. Is that a yes?" Jordan needed to be sure.

"Yes," Aaron replied with another kiss and a single tear in the corner of his eye.

"All right, guys, time to jump," Dana told them. "Jordan, secure your harnesses."

Jordan stood and clipped himself and Aaron together in five places. "He's not going anywhere." He opened the hatch and said against Aaron's ear, "You gotta jump. The parachute and I are right behind you."

Aaron took a breath and stepped off the plane into the cold December sky. The wind rushed in their faces. Translucent clouds only briefly broke up the view of the rapidly approaching ground. "Jordan, the parachute!"

"Not yet."

"We're falling!" Aaron screamed.

"We jumped from a plane. What do you expect?" Jordan asked over the roar of the drop as he hugged him and kissed his cheek. "We're going to fall for another thirty seconds. Trust me and breathe. Let go."

Aaron pulled in a shaky breath and released it slowly. "Oh, God."

"Scary. Exciting. And then—" Jordan deployed the parachute. "—comforting," he finished. "Spread your arms and fly, Angel."

"Shit. God. Shit," Aaron chanted, his breathing settling incrementally. "It's beautiful."

"That too," Jordan said. "I can loosen the connection to—"

"Don't you dare," Aaron called. "Also, I'm not sure it was fair to propose before we jumped out of a plane with my means of survival on your back."

"Would your answer have been different on the ground?" Jordan asked.

"Uh-uh."

They careened in silence until they made a soft landing on the drop zone, surrounded by their families and friends. Jordan unzipped the pack and held up a sign reading "HE SAID YES!" and the small crowd erupted in applause.

Aaron blushed, kissed Jordan, and whispered, "You are such a sap."

Chapter Twelve

SEPTEMBER 2013, LANGLEY, VIRGINIA

Goddamn nightmare. Aaron trembled at his desk. *Get it together. People are staring.* Aaron lifted his coffee cup as he refreshed his email. The caffeine assisted in keeping his eyes open but did nothing to help the shaking. Not that Aaron honestly believed he'd sleep, anyway. After he'd dreamed two nights ago that Jordan had been dragged off and thrown in a prison cell by enemy troops, sleep became impossible. Aaron checked his phone again, also futile. Jordan had said he might not be in contact for a few days. Why was Aaron letting a dream fuck with his head so much? It didn't make sense.

"Collins, may I have a word with you?" Aaron's supervisor, Mick Keller, requested.

Oh, crap. I've been noticeably slacking off. "Of course, sir," Aaron replied, pushing his chair out.

"You may want to pack your things, since you'll be allowed to go home after we talk," Keller told him.

There's no way I've been lazy enough for him to send me home. "Is there a problem with my performance?"

"No, your performance is always satisfactory, Collins. Please follow me." Keller waited for Aaron to place his netbook, cell phone, and file in his bag before leading him to the elevator.

Where are we going? Aaron wondered as the elevator descended to the basement. He tried to remember what was in the basement. *Conference rooms. Right.* His heart picked up speed when the elevator doors slid open to reveal Troy and two other military officers in dress uniforms at the end of the hall. The dread that had sent it into overdrive dropped his heart to his gut. Aaron compelled his feet to move forward alongside Keller.

When Troy completed the introductions of Captain Pyrilli and Colonel Bryant, Keller excused himself. "Please have a seat." LTC Bryant addressed the people gathered.

And suddenly, Aaron understood. They were here to talk to him about the nightmare. "I'll stand," he said.

"You really need to sit," Troy told him.

"No, I need to get back to work. Please tell me what you came here to tell me," Aaron responded.

"You won't be going back to work today, Mr. Collins. Please sit down," Colonel Bryant repeated, and Aaron took the seat that Troy pulled out.

"What happened to Jordan?" Aaron asked. Bryant and Pyrilli leaned back with wide eyes. "What? Am I not supposed to have figured out that three military officers in dress uniforms mean bad news?"

"Captain Collins served his country with the highest honor." Bryant began what Aaron predicted to be a very long speech that would still not answer his question.

Aaron raised his hand to stop the lieutenant colonel from continuing about Jordan's bravery for another twenty minutes. "I know that my husband is a great soldier and a respected leader. Did something go wrong with his latest mission?"

"What do you know about his mission?" Pyrilli asked.

After massaging his temples, Aaron responded, "Nothing new, except that he was tired and stressed the last few weeks. He told me two days ago that he would be incommunicado. Your turn."

"I beg your pardon?" Colonel Bryant inquired.

This man is deliberately annoying me. Aaron massaged harder. "What do you know?"

"Captain Collins and Lieutenant Parks met with prominent members of the Afghanistan grand council regarding the release of the American POWs. In the process of saving the lives of fifteen American soldiers, unfortunately, Captain Collins lost his. I'm sorry for your loss," Bryant explained.

Aaron's gaze fell to his tattoo on the inside of his arm. And waited for the sadness to overcome him. But no. "Where is he?"

"Excuse me?" the LTC pressed.

"Do you need a hearing aid?"

"Aaron!" Troy exclaimed.

"I thought those were both valid questions, sorry. Where is Jordan?" Aaron asked again.

"We were not able to recover a body," Bryant replied. "The area is under fire, which means—"

"There's a current battle going on. I understand," Aaron told them, losing patience with the whole thing. "How can you claim a death without a body?"

"They found his dog tags and burned uniform in the rubble of the prison building," Troy cut in, placing a hand on Aaron's arm. "No one is taking this lightly."

"Obviously, they're not taking it as seriously as they should, or else they'd have a body or maybe a picture of a body. Do you have that?" Aaron demanded of Colonel Bryant.

"We already explained that the area is under fire. It isn't safe to go digging around," Pyrilli told him. "I'm sorry, but everyone who was left in the building is dead."

"Fine, then prove to me he was in the building," Aaron responded.

"We have eyewitness accounts of the freed POWs who all said they saw him." Bryant wiped his brow. "As terrible as it is, sometimes soldiers have to pay the ultimate price. Captain Collins would want you to accept his death with dignity. He will be honored in a military funeral, receiving medals of service, in addition to the promotion he is owed, posthumously."

"No. Jordan would want me to make sure you turned over every sand dune in the Middle East until you find him." Aaron stood up and strode toward the door. "Another thing, I'm the next of kin. I will not approve a promotion." With that, Aaron left the room. A promotion to major would extend Jordan's service once he was found. And Aaron would find him. One way or another.

Chapter Thirteen

HOURS LATER—AARON lost track of how many—he clicked through the tenth news report on the freeing of the POWs, remembering what Jordan always said about the media: "Only pay attention to the facts." So far, the facts included twenty original POWs, five of whom were killed before Jordan and Doug Parks got involved. Then, according to consensus, Jordan and Doug freed the remaining fifteen and were killed in the process. No one had any bodies. Aaron growled at the sound of a knock on the door. All damn day people had been calling, texting, and otherwise bothering Aaron. The person outside knocked louder.

"Aaron, it's Troy. Open up."

"I'm busy," Aaron responded without moving.

"I could get a warrant."

Aaron stormed over and threw the door open. "What exactly would you have me arrested for?" he demanded, gaze flitting to the army duffel bag and a pizza box.

"Search warrant," Troy corrected. "And I'm sure I would come up with something." He put his foot in the doorframe before Aaron could close it. "I'm sorry. Please let me talk."

"Whatever." Aaron moved out of the way. "Talk, but you leave when I've heard enough."

"That's fine." Troy set the duffel bag on the side of the couch. "Have you eaten?"

"Not hungry," Aaron replied, crossing his arms over his chest and staring down at Troy, who had the nerve to smirk.

"You're not as scary as you think. Maybe if you were shaped less like a flagpole, people might be intimidated."

"If you're here to make fun of me, you can leave." Aaron sat back on the couch with his computer.

Troy shook his head. "I came to bring you Jordan's personal effects and to try to convince you to eat."

"I can't eat. My stomach is a mess." Aaron swallowed past the lump in his throat at the term "personal effects."

"I understand. This is the hardest news for any loved one to hear."

"Especially when it's not true." Aaron refreshed the page in hopes of receiving new results.

"Aaron—" Troy started, but Aaron cut him off.

"You said you wanted to be my friend. You promised you would listen to me. You cannot do that if you go into a conversation thinking you already know better." Aaron rubbed his tattoo.

"Part of being a friend is helping the other person to face reality with dignity. Unfortunately, this is your new reality. Jordan is—"

"Lost in the sand dunes because the people he risked his life for didn't stop to search for him." Aaron took a deep breath. "I am not unrealistic. I fully comprehend the risks Jordan faced every day. So does he. We had many conversations about how to handle that news. You know what step one is?"

"Scream? Cry? Either is acceptable," Troy assured him.

"No. Identify his body. If I can't identify him with my naked eye, then I insist on a DNA analysis. Because even commanding officers fuck up." Aaron swept his hair back. "I am not going to mourn my husband without actual proof he's dead. Do you have any?"

Troy opened a zipper pocket on the duffel bag and passed Aaron Jordan's dog tags. "They found these close to his uniform."

Aaron threw them on the ground. "That fucking silver chain is not proof of anything!" He rubbed his face and jumped to his feet to pace the living room.

"Bryant said it would be too dangerous to look any further, but Jordan could not have survived the fire," Troy said.

"Maybe he didn't. I accept that possibility. I do not accept it as a fact without some hard proof. Besides," Aaron added quietly. "No one would have to tell me if he had died. I would know."

"You can't demand logic and matching emotions," Troy answered.

"Sure, I can, because my gut has never once steered me wrong with him. And if you're asking me to go against my instincts, then I need proof. Will you help? Please?"

Troy patted the seat next to him. Aaron sat as Troy spoke. "I will help, but you have to be practical. Most people won't believe you. And calling high-ranking military officers liars won't win you any friends."

"Don't care."

Wrapping an arm around Aaron's waist, Troy said, "Your boss might. Bryant lodged a complaint with Keller."

Aaron stiffened and moved away. "Troy, I am not ready for cuddling."

"Sorry, I thought you could use some comfort. It won't happen again, unless you change your mind."

Don't count on it. Aaron sensed Troy's eyes boring into his back as he moved across the room to grab his notebook containing the search results, plus the information he had on the case beforehand. "This is what I've found so far."

"Aaron, you were wrong about one thing. They can hold a funeral without your consent by taking expenses from his life insurance before giving you the remainder," Troy told him.

Aaron blinked over at him. "What are they burying? There's no body."

"Um, a casket with his toe tags and burned uniform. The public doesn't need to know there isn't a body," Troy explained. "It's better for everyone if there's a sense of closure."

Aaron gritted his teeth. "I am definitely not going and lying to our friends, family, and colleagues."

"People will think you don't respect him," Troy offered.

"Then they should ask me. I would be happy to tell them that I love, honor, and respect my husband enough to not give up on him."

"I hope you don't regret that."

Aaron nudged the notebook toward him. "Please try to fill in the gaps for me."

AFTER TROY LEFT several hours later, another knock sounded at the door. Aaron swung it open, assuming the officer had forgotten something but found Jordan's father on the other side. Aaron swallowed as he met the elderly man's red eyes. "May I come in?" Elliot asked when they stood there staring at each other for a few moments.

"Of course. I'm sorry." Aaron moved out of the way and noted his careful steps to the couch. "Can I get you something to drink?"

"Not quite yet. I would like to speak with you."

Aaron took a seat across from him. All right, he could admit to being a coward. He should have approached Elliot first, but what was he going to say?

"Who was that?" Elliot asked.

"Huh?"

"The man who just left. He had been here several hours."

"You've been watching the whole time?"

"I came by to talk to you after the army officers left my house but found myself at a loss for words. I planned to wait in my car until I got my emotions under control, but then that man pulled up and stayed into the evening. Who is he? I'm asking for a reason, Aaron. Please be honest."

Keeping eye contact, Aaron replied, "That's General Troy Hart. He's a friend. I'm hoping that he can help me find out what happened to Jordan."

"You aren't being unfaithful, then?"

"Never." Aaron blinked a few times, then prodded, "Why do you ask?"

Elliot gave him a sad smile. "I had an interesting visit from some very high-ranking army officials. They had quite the story to share."

"I don't believe it," Aaron said.

"Yes, I heard." His smile now contained some amusement. "Why?"

Aaron inhaled, seeking the courage he had when talking to Troy, Bryant, and Pyrilli. "Why should I? Because someone in an expensive suit says so? I need more than that, Elliot."

Elliot nodded slowly. "You think Jordan survived the fire."

"I...think there's a possibility. And I will continue to believe that until they prove me wrong. I'm sorry if you think that's disrespectful to the army officers, but I think they're disrespecting Jordan by not searching for him." Not that Aaron expected agreement from Elliot. He considered sharing his dream as evidence for his doubts, but it wouldn't improve Elliot's perception of his sanity.

"They asked me to come here and tell you to fall in line. Do as you're told. I informed them that God himself could not accomplish that feat, and I was far too old and feeble to try."

Aaron let a surprised laugh escape. "You are far from feeble." Though Elliot had been aging more rapidly since his wife died. "Do you believe what they said about Jordan?"

Elliot shrugged. "I don't know. And I wouldn't have any idea where to begin questioning them. Thirty-five years of following orders and internalizing messages of duty and justice take a toll on a person's free thought. I'm glad you and Jordan have avoided those messages to some degree. I won't badger you about protocol if you promise me two things." He waited for Aaron to meet his gaze again before continuing, "Don't make the search too public, and keep me updated. I want to know if you find anything out."

"Of course. Thank you for understanding," Aaron said.

Elliot nodded again. "Thank you for questioning when I couldn't. Oh, and, Aaron, I appreciate that nights get cold when your spouse is so far from you, but if you don't mind me saying, if you need some extra warmth, you could do better than a naked mole rat."

Aaron's cheeks heated. "That is not something you need to worry about."

Chapter Fourteen

SEPTEMBER 2013, KABUL, AFGHANISTAN

"Angel," Jordan moaned. "Stop, please, that hurts."

"I'm sorry," a female voice said in Farsi. "I'm trying to be gentle."

Female? Farsi? What the fuck is going on? Jordan yanked his leg away from the Afghan woman, which sent a shot of pain through him. "Ow! Fuck!"

"Can you understand me?" she asked. Jordan barely nodded. "My name is Adeela Nadar. I'm a nurse."

Nadar... Jordan racked his foggy brain for why that name sounded familiar. *Fuck. The Afghanistan official. That makes Adeela...enemy's wife.* "Should you be here?" he asked in her native tongue.

"My job," she answered simply. "I need to clean your ankle. See if the dog broke it."

"Dog?" Jordan glanced down at his feet. The ankle that had been previously injured was split open and bleeding from the joint.

"Don't puke. Or warn me and I'll get you a bag. You have pins in here. What happened?"

"Shot during my first deployment," Jordan told her. "Adeela, will you get in trouble for being here? Will I?" Middle Eastern men were possessive of their women to the point that it could cost both the women, and the men they were caught alone with, their lives.

"No, I was ordered to clean you up," she said. "Dead prisoners are too quiet."

Jordan leaned his head back. Prisoner. Now, he understood. "Where are the other American prisoners?"

"Free. The lieutenant is quiet," Adeela responded. "Sorry."

"I'm guessing you didn't pull the trigger." Jordan hissed in pain as she moved his foot. "What dog bit me?"

Adeela smirked. "Her name's Sweetie. Guard dog."

"Why am I alive if Lieutenant Parks is dead?"

"Anwar believed you had more information, but your government thinks you are dead as well."

"So, you're making sure I'm healed before they execute me?"

Adeela motioned to the tattoo on Jordan's inner arm. "Angel wouldn't appreciate that, would she?"

He shook his head and clamped his mouth shut before he corrected Angel's gender. For as much as Jordan was out and proud at home, due to his common sense, he tended not to mention it in the Middle East. "Is it broken?" he questioned, indicating his ankle.

"Without an X-ray, my best guess is yes. I can fix it, but..."

"But...what?" She answered Jordan's question by holding up a bottle of the Middle Eastern ibuprofen. "Oh, no, Adeela, that's barely enough to keep me from going into shock with the pain I have now. You can't set a bone with 600 mg of ibuprofen." The dog would have been a less painful way to die. At least he'd been properly drugged for that.

Adeela blinked at him for a long moment, then said, "You whine a lot for a soldier. Don't they train you to handle unfavorable physical conditions in the United States?"

Jordan laughed and, for the first time, noticed the tightness in his chest. "And you cause a lot of pain for a nurse. Do you always assist with the torture?"

Her eyes clouded. "Never. I help the prisoners when they let me. Many won't because I have too many X chromosomes or wear the wrong uniform."

"Bet those aren't the same people," Jordan replied softly.

She smiled at him and pulled out a vodka bottle and a shot glass. "Better?"

Jordan returned the smile. Though he had no reason to, he trusted Adeela's words. Her eyes told Jordan that she had the best intentions. He had no way to judge her medical training. "You can keep the glass."

As he washed the pills down with half the bottle of vodka, Adeela set up the "operating table" with a scalpel, water, black cloth, and something that looked like a medical hammer. "You can scream. No one can hear you here."

Jordan was about to ask exactly where "here" was, but then she started working on his ankle. The pain consumed his being. The last thing he heard was a ringing phone before welcoming the blackness from the shock.

TWO YEARS EARLIER, BETHESDA, MARYLAND

"Mm, I hate that ringtone," Jordan groaned, forcing an eye open. "Who would call at 1:00 a.m.?" he mused. *If work wanted me, they'd call my cell, no? Parents too.*

"Answer. You'll find out who's on the other line and the ringing stops. It's a great system," Aaron grumbled.

"Hello?" Jordan said into the cordless receiver.

"Good evening, sir. My name is Officer James Henry, from the Montgomery Village police force. May I please speak with Captain Jordan Collins?" the man on the other line said in a rush.

"Speaking. How can I help you, Officer?" At Jordan's words, Aaron turned on the light and wrapped an arm around his shoulders.

"I'm sorry to inform you..."

Jordan only heard bits and pieces of the policeman's speech. His parents. Drunk driver. Car crash. Dead. "A-are you sure?" he asked, annoyed at his trembling voice.

"Yes, please come" was all Jordan heard.

"Thank you. I'll be right there," Jordan promised and set the phone on its receiver. "Maybe the police are wrong. It's happened before."

Aaron hugged him tightly. "Maybe. Let's take one step at a time." He kissed Jordan's head. "I love you. We're in this together."

"I love you too." Jordan gave him another hug, then stood on his aching ankle. *Must be raining*, he thought and listened for the beat of raindrops on the roof. Instead he heard rolling thunder in the distance. Even worse for the pins in his ankle. He dressed in silence as Aaron used the bathroom and came out with prescription-strength ibuprofen.

"Heard the thunder," Aaron explained.

The gesture pricked Jordan's eyes with the tears he had been suppressing. "What would I do without you?"

Aaron took his hand, grabbed the keys to his SUV, and led Jordan outside. "You will never have to find out."

As soon as they were in the car, a flash of lightning split the booming sky. Water flew from the clouds, fleeing the noise and light. Jordan intertwined his fingers with Aaron's as Aaron drove forty-five minutes through the storm toward the hospital in his hometown, where the officer said he'd meet them.

Jordan recognized the last sign before they reached the hospital and his heart sped up. "Angel, stop!" Aaron pulled into a McDonald's parking lot, and Jordan ran inside, barely feeling the sting of the angry rain. The smell of french fries turned his stomach, which he emptied into the first stall of the bathroom. Nothing about this was right. His parents should be home in their bed. Why would they be out so late? Maybe...someone stole their wallets and called Jordan for...what? Money? A prank? Why didn't he think to call them? His breath came in short spurts, and though he swore his stomach was empty, retching brought more vomit. The heaves turned dry, and he sank to the dirty floor.

"Sir?" a woman asked from the door.

"I will buy something on my way out," he responded, his eyes still shut.

"Um, no, you're in the women's room," she hedged.

I'm...what? Jordan opened his eyes and looked around. Up until this point, he hadn't noticed the pink walls or metal containers for feminine products. He sighed, flushed the toilet, and hoisted himself up off the floor. "I'm sorry," he told the employee. "I didn't mean..."

She smiled kindly at him and patted his shoulder after he washed his hands. "Your husband explained the situation to me. I just didn't want to make a female customer uncomfortable, should she try to use the restroom."

Jordan thanked her and ducked under the doorway, where Aaron leaned against the opposite wall. "I'm not helping the stereotype of gays as feminine," Jordan said.

Aaron offered a small smile. "I think the leaders of the cause will forgive you. Are you all right?"

"No. I think I'm finished puking though." Jordan ran his hands over his face, sticky from tears. "We can leave after I clean up." He exhaled and walked into the men's room, checking the door twice on his way. The mirror reflected a pale, blotchy-faced man that Jordan almost didn't recognize. His tan skin rarely showed fatigue or illness. He couldn't force his smile. And for some reason, he felt like he should try. "I didn't call them," Jordan told Aaron.

"What?" Aaron asked, wetting a paper towel and washing Jordan's face. "You talked to your parents three or four times a week. No one would accuse you of being uncommunicative."

"Tonight. After the police called to say they died, I didn't try to reach them, even though the police could be wrong. Why?" Jordan didn't resist Aaron's help.

Aaron kissed him deeply and threw away the paper towel. "Because I think you're intuitive enough to know that there was no mistake. You have the gift of connection with people you care about."

Some gift. Jordan sighed once more as Aaron held him. For the most part, though, it was.

"Ready?" Aaron asked after a few minutes.

"As I'll ever be," he responded. Jordan shook hands with the cop and the coroner upon their arrival at the hospital.

"Would you like to see your mother or father first?" the policeman asked.

Jordan blinked at him and then at Aaron. "Aren't they together?"

"No, your father is in the ICU," the cop explained.

Aaron took Jordan's hand. "And his mother?"

"Was killed instantly. I'm sorry," the coroner answered.

"Is my father stable?" Jordan's mind whirred. What kind of accident would spare one of them, but not the other? He really should have paid more attention to the original phone call.

"Yes, he will be moved to a regular room after the doctors get some test results back," the officer said.

"All right, then I should see my mom first." The two men offered their silent agreement.

On the elevator ride down to the morgue, Jordan squeezed courage from Aaron's hand. The chill as the group stepped off the elevator went right to Jordan's bones. The morgue was painted white and lined with stainless-steel doors, and heavy with sulfate. A body lay on the far table under a white sheet.

"We've prepared her for you," the morgue technician told him. "Please tell me if you recognize this woman."

Jordan made it across the room, though he didn't remember walking there. Nor did he believe he could if challenged to do so.

"Is this your mother?" the technician asked, pulling back the sheets covering the corpse's face.

No. This woman is cold and covered in blood. She's not the same woman who adopted, encouraged, and loved me every day. "Yes."

"I'm sorry," Officer Henry responded. "We'll leave you two alone with her. Take as much time as you need. When you're ready, we'll show you to your father."

"I don't need time."

"Are you sure?" Aaron asked.

"There's no point." Jordan squeezed his hand again. "Please, Angel." Aaron nodded at the cop and hospital worker, who led them out. After Jordan signed the papers, the policeman led them upstairs to his father's door.

"I'll wait here," Aaron told him.

"No, come with me, please," Jordan begged.

"He'll want—"

"His family. We're it now," Jordan replied. Aaron followed him in. Elliot stared up at the ceiling, with only one bandage across his cheek. "Hey, Dad."

Elliot turned his head. "Hi, boys. You should go home to bed. There's nothing you can do here." They both sat down. "You don't listen very well. How'd you survive basic?"

The words were heavy with anguish, so Jordan ignored the insult. "How are you feeling?"

"Wonderful."

"You're a worse liar than I am," Jordan informed him.

"Then don't ask stupid questions." Elliot blew out a breath. "How do I feel? Worthless."

"Dad, you're not—"

"The hell I'm not!" Elliot fisted the sheets and calmed his breathing. "From the moment I met your mother, everything I did was to make her happy and protect you both. I went to war with one thing on my mind—keeping my family safe at all costs. That is what I risked my life for day in and day out. Then tonight I wound up in oncoming traffic. I don't know how. I don't remember doing it. All I know is that the woman who spent forty years by my side is dead because of something I did." Elliot faced the other way again.

Aaron kissed the back of Jordan's hand and said, "No, a truck driver ran a red light. It was not your fault."

Did Aaron see the police report? Hell, maybe I saw it and wasn't paying attention.

"I still should have—"

Aaron shook his head. "Nothing. You did everything right. You swerved away from the truck, called 911, and assisted the EMTs. There was no one better for Marie to be in the car with." He patted Elliot's blanket-covered arm and said, "Even if it didn't turn out the way you hoped, you protected her the best way anyone could."

Jordan steeled his own emotions to comfort his father as best he could.

Chapter Fifteen

SEPTEMBER 2013, KABUL, AFGHANISTAN

"Ugh." Jordan slit his eyes open to see Adeela dabbing a washcloth over his forehead, her face creased with concern.

"You're awake." She sat back on her heels. "I was worried."

It took Jordan a second to translate her words from Farsi. "Why? Did the surgery go poorly?"

"Surgery was four days ago," she answered. "You haven't woken up until now. That's not good."

Jordan rubbed his face and sat up against the wall. "No. It's not. Why didn't you take me to a hospital?"

Adeela looked at the ground. "I'm sorry. I don't get to make that decision."

Knowing he couldn't touch her because of Islamic law, Jordan craned his neck to catch her gaze. "I understand. Thank you for taking care of me."

"Of course," she answered. "I do the best I can."

Jordan straightened his back. "I believe that." He turned his head and coughed violently. "That's blood."

"Yes, it is," Adeela said, cleaning his hand with an alcohol pad. "Have you had a tuberculosis shot?"

Fuck. He shook his head. "I'm allergic to the vaccine. I get hives."

"Hives are better than tuberculosis, in my experience."

"Not if they close your throat," Jordan replied. As he became more awake, the pain in his ankle intensified until it radiated throughout his body. He squeezed his eyes and breathed slowly.

"I will try to get you an antibiotic," Adeela promised. "Hopefully, it's only pneumonia."

Never thought I'd wish for pneumonia. But she's right; it is the better alternative. "Thank you. Is the TB the reason for my whole body aching?"

"No...the guards tried to wake you up with clubs... I'm sorry," Adeela answered. "I tried to stop them, but..."

Jordan shook his head. "Please don't get yourself hurt on my account."

"They aren't following the rules. We aren't North Korea."

No. That was the one place in the world Jordan would want to be less than where he was. Their prison camps were unlike anything the world had seen since the Nazis. "Where are we?" he asked without opening his eyes.

"Prison in Shar-e-Naw."

"How'd that happen?" They had been on the other side of Kabul for the meeting with the Afghan officials.

"Americans burned the prison when their officers were killed." The nurse checked Jordan's wounds as they talked.

"Why do they think I'm dead?"

"Your security told them the lieutenant was shot and you were burned alive. They have your burned uniforms and dog tags."

Jordan opened his eyes again at the anger in Adeela's voice and the ridiculousness of her words. *That is not sufficient evidence of death... Wait. It is if the area was under fire. Fuck.* They wouldn't look for him if they thought he was dead. Jordan concentrated on his breathing to settle the panic that only now hit him. He could fix this. "Can you get me a Geneva Convention card to send to my government?"

"I will ask."

"That shouldn't be a problem. Nadar is supposed to give those cards to any POW who requests them."

"I know what he's supposed to do," she answered, each word containing more venom than the last.

The increased tension in the room prompted him to ask, "Who are you mad at?" Though Jordan was positive it was the Americans.

"Everyone. The leaders. Mine. Yours. They're all being stupid and treating life as useless," she ranted, but suddenly calmed and met his gaze. "I knew of you during your last deployment."

"I'm sorry. I don't remember us meeting."

"We didn't. You refused to run an aid mission. I was so relieved," she told him, and he tilted his head to the side. "The Taliban knew about your plans. They planted suicide bombers—myself included—among the poor. But when the Americans never showed up, the bombers went home. You saved my life. I will do my best to save yours."

Jordan smiled. "Thank you. Can I ask one more question?"

"Sure."

"I have never known an Afghan woman who looks me in the eye and speaks plainly," Jordan said.

"Not a question, but I'll answer it this way: I have never known an American soldier not to leer at me or insult my intelligence with condescension." Adeela returned the smile and handed him cold broth and water. "Try to finish that before I come back in a few hours. And keep your foot up."

Jordan offered his silent agreement as he stretched out on the concrete bed. Whether or not he got the Geneva card, he still had to find a way out. He had a life to return to.

ONE YEAR EARLIER, BETHESDA, MARYLAND

Jordan woke up ready to complain about Aaron stealing his covers but decided against it when he saw his fiancé kneeling between his legs. "Good morning, Angel."

"Mm, I'm going to make sure it is," he promised as he leaned down to take Jordan's cock in his mouth.

"Oh," Jordan moaned as Aaron sucked his length in all at once and swirled his tongue from the base to the tip on the way out. He bobbed his head up and down, massaging Jordan with his mouth until he cried out in orgasm. "You win."

Aaron sat back on his heels and licked the stray fluid from his lips. "Nope," he said and handed him a newspaper. "We won."

Jordan blinked at the circled headline: "Don't Ask, Don't Tell Repealed!" He grinned and extended his arms. He had known it was coming but seeing it in print gave his heart wings.

Aaron embraced him quickly. "Still want to marry me?"

"Will you wake me up like that every day?"

"No, and I'll continue to steal your covers," Aaron replied.

"Then I'll continue to stick my cold feet between your warm legs." Jordan laughed and kissed him. "When should we do it?"

Aaron folded himself between Jordan's legs and snuggled with him. "Captain Barry Lysander is meeting us at Anacostia Park at noon on Saturday."

"Awesome!" Jordan laughed again. "Except we both have work."

"No again. We have a week's vacation, starting today. I know because I requested it," Aaron informed him.

"You talked to the lieutenant colonel to request my vacation?" Jordan clarified. "Did you tell him why?"

"Didn't have to. I was the third person to request time off around the planned repeal."

"Why Saturday?"

"Three days waiting for a marriage license." Aaron kissed him lightly. "So today we go apply and have all the sex we can between now and Saturday, when it becomes boring."

Jordan nipped Aaron's neck and squeezed him tight. "Sex hasn't been boring even once in ten years. I highly doubt pledging to love each other forever will change that."

Aaron sighed dramatically. "So, you don't want to have crazy sex for three straight days? Already it starts!"

Capturing Aaron's lips, Jordan unfolded him and flipped him onto his back to begin proving him wrong.

Chapter Sixteen

SEPTEMBER 2013, BETHESDA, MARYLAND

The banging on the front door cut through the music blaring through Aaron's headphones on the day of Jordan's funeral. He tore his eyes from the computer screen to the door. Aaron's phone had been ringing since the officers broke the news about Jordan's "death." The phone he could ignore, but the door was harder, at least with the curtains pushed to the side. *I have to remember to close those.* The banging continued. "All right! I'm coming," he shouted and threw open the door to find his brother on the other side.

"You're wearing that?" Chris asked.

"Sorry, I would have changed into my fancy sweatpants if I wasn't avoiding people," Aaron replied.

"I haven't been able to get in touch with you for days."

"Avoiding people. You look an awful lot like a person." Aaron stepped aside so his brother could come in. "Wait a second. What are *you* wearing?"

"A suit. That's what you wear to funerals," Chris told him. "Why aren't you?"

"Because I'm not going to a funeral, which I already told you." Aaron returned to his desk.

"I thought you were kidding." Chris stood in front of the desk.

Aaron refreshed his email, hoping to hear back from a CIA contact. "You can't intimidate me, Chris. You still wet the bed."

"That was once!" Chris huffed, and Aaron lifted his eyebrows. "Only when I drink too much. That isn't the point!"

"It's my point. You're standing above me, probably thinking what you say will carry more weight, but the knowledge that you wet the bed kills any chance of you scaring me into changing my behavior." Aaron focused back on his empty email inbox.

"You...aren't going to your husband's funeral?"

"No."

"Why?"

How many times do I have to explain this? I must be on the hundredth. Maybe I should look into making a recording for whenever someone asks that damn question. "Because I have no reason to believe Jordan is dead, and until I do, I'm a lot more useful here trying to find him than sitting in a stuffy church."

Chris sat on the couch next to Aaron's chair and placed his hand on his arm. "Aaron, are you okay?"

"Sure."

"I know this is difficult for you, but..."

Aaron waved him off. "Don't give me the denial speech. I have it memorized."

"This is the very definition of denial," Chris said. "You're saying Jordan isn't dead..."

Aaron sighed. "If people are going to ask me the same questions over and over, I really wish one of them would listen to the response. I never said he wasn't dead. I said I couldn't *believe* he was dead until I got some proof. Dog tags are not proof."

"The building he was in burned to the ground."

"Yes, it did. Answer me this: How did the soldiers find his dog tags and burned uniform without uncovering his body? Did he throw off the chain and strip as he suffocated from the carbon dioxide?" Aaron received a blank expression from his brother. "Didn't make sense to me either."

"Don't you think the military has a system so mistakes like this don't happen?"

Aaron shook his head. "Do you know what I do for a living? I'm an eyewitness to how fucked up our government is. And if you think any system we live under is flawless, then I finally understand how you keep falling for those get-rich-quick schemes."

After staring at him for a long moment, Chris stood up again. "I never thought I would see the day where I was the more responsible one of us. I hope you change your mind."

"I won't," Aaron promised. "Not unless someone proves my logic wrong."

"This isn't logic," Chris said. "It's wishful thinking."

"Sometimes I wonder if you know me at all."

"Obviously, I don't. The brother I knew loved his husband enough to pay his respects even if it was hard."

"Funny. I love and respect my husband enough to bring him home. I'm the only one who can do it, since everyone is going to cry over an empty casket. Make sure the door's shut tight on your way out; the lock's been loose."

"Waiting for Jordan to fix it?" Chris tossed back.

"You know what? Maybe I will." Aaron fitted the headphones on his ears.

Two hours later, he forced himself to get up and make food because his stomach growled louder than his music, and he didn't need a headache on top of everything else. Aaron spread mustard on two pieces of bread as the front door handle jiggled. Before he could react, his father entered the house. *Guess I'm getting a headache anyway.*

"Let me save you the trouble of a lecture. I should go to Jordan's funeral to prove I love and respect him."

"No. You go to the funeral because you respect yourself."

Aaron shook his head and turned back to his sandwich. "We have different definitions of respect. You can see yourself out."

"What will people say?"

"Probably that I'm an uncaring asshole. You still haven't left."

"I'm not leaving without you."

"You're missing it too, then," Aaron threw back. "Go. I have work to do."

"Look, I realize you and Jordan were fighting before his mission," Karl started.

"What are you talking about?" Aaron faced his father again.

"Chris told me you have been seeing someone else, which I don't blame you for. I hear Korean men don't have much in the way of size, but—"

"Stop. That's bullshit. Chris saw me with a friend from work. You can have those without sleeping with the other person. I realize that you have no experience with this concept, but it does happen." Aaron picked up his plate and strode past his father. Karl changed secretaries at his construction business every time one of them wanted more from him than the added perks he offered. "And you know nothing about my relationship with Jordan."

"Don't bother sitting down, young man." Karl's words rang with a haughtiness Aaron had not heard since he was a teenager. "I don't care about your so-called relationship. It's over anyway. You are to go upstairs and put your black suit on."

Aaron's face heated, his anger coloring his cheeks. "Or you'll what?"

Karl advanced toward him. "Carry you up and do it myself. Then I will carry you out to the car and sit with you in the church to make sure you pay your respects."

"You will do nothing except leave. I don't ever want to hear from you again. You do not get to come into my house and make judgments about my marriage. Because let me tell you something, you aren't half the man Jordan is, and you never will be."

"Dead? Someday I will be."

Not soon enough. Aaron picked up his cell and dialed nine. "Get the fuck out before I finish this phone number." He didn't bother to look up when the door slammed.

OCTOBER 2013, AFGHANISTAN

Adeela turned the key in the lock of Jordan's cell and exclaimed, "I brought you presents!"

Jordan gave a smile that may have come out more pained than he intended. But it was difficult to share in her excitement when his body throbbed. "Yeah? Antibiotics in there?"

She cast her eyes down. "We can't treat until we know what it is."

"The last time you were here you were leaning toward pneumonia. What changed?" Jordan questioned, suppressing a cough.

Adeela sat down next to him. "I gave you that bucket for a reason. Your body is trying to expel the germs."

"Yes, well, it's not pretty." This time the convulsion in Jordan's chest forced the bloody mucus out into the silver bucket. Once it passed, he wiped his mouth and set the bucket down.

"People hoping to be surrounded by pretty things don't join the army or become nurses." Adeela reached toward his face, touched the back of her hand to his forehead and cheeks, and smiled. "You're not as warm, at least. But being polite about getting rid of germs is not smart."

He returned the smile. "Why are you doubting your diagnosis?"

"I'm not, but Anwar does not agree that you need antibiotics."

The corners of his mouth fell. "Does he have to?"

"For medicine, yes." Adeela placed a bag of pills in his hand. "Percocet. Won't cure anything, but it might make it easier to bear."

That was a scary proposition for Jordan. If all he treated was the pain, he'd become dependent. At the same time, improving the pain might allow him to sleep. "Thank you," he said. "Did Anwar send the Geneva Convention card?"

She glanced up. "I gave him the card you filled out."

Jordan's attempt at a slow exhale turned to a fit of coughs. "Damn it."

"I'm sorry."

"It's not even close to your fault." All the more reason for him to escape. "Did you bring the map?" Adeela opened a folded piece of paper, which Jordan studied. He figured out how to escape the compound, when the guards changed shifts. The challenge lay in getting from the prison to the American Embassy. "Do any of the deliveries to the prison correspond with shift changes?"

"No, but you would only have to wait about twenty minutes between leaving and the truck coming," Adeela answered.

Twenty minutes to hide in the desert is far from ideal. Jordan started drawing on a blank sheet of paper.

"What are you doing?"

"Copying my route to memorize it," he told her. "I don't want to slow down to check the map every hundred yards." It occurred to him that if Adeela told anyone his plans, he would be dead in minutes. Jordan had to go with his gut instinct that she could be trusted. Otherwise, he had no chance of surviving.

"Jordan, where are your parents from?" Adeela asked, seemingly out of the blue.

He lifted his gaze from the paper in surprise. "America."

"No, I mean...their parents." She shifted next to him.

"You're asking my ethnicity?" She nodded. "The orphanage where my parents adopted me from guessed that my sperm donor was of African descent and my egg donor from Korean."

Adeela opened and closed her mouth several times before saying, "Would you consider...? No, never mind."

"Would I consider what?" he prodded.

Adeela sighed. "Wearing an Afghanistan army uniform."

Yeah. That would go over so well with the American embassy, especially since I no longer have my ID. "I don't think that's such a great idea."

She chewed her lip. "You don't look the same as people here. That's okay in America. But we don't have Korean African people in Afghanistan."

"A uniform isn't going to change my skin color."

"No, but a hat could shade your face and make you stand out less," she explained.

"Your government is supposed to have given me an American uniform," Jordan protested, to which Adeela rolled her eyes and stood to pace.

"Yes. And sent your Geneva Convention card. And give you proper food and medicine I asked for. The government was supposed to do all of those things, but it didn't. Your government was supposed to break their backs looking for you, but they didn't do that either. Are you going to allow their incompetence stop you from surviving?"

Jordan's jaw dropped. He could talk about the reasons the US didn't look harder for him, but they didn't matter. "What's to stop the US MPs from shooting me for showing up unannounced in an Afghan uniform? They think I'm dead. I don't know that I'm going to get a chance to explain otherwise."

Adeela turned toward him again. "What if you didn't go to the embassy?"

"Then I can't get home," he answered. "I have no passport, no money, and no connections here."

"If you could get home without going to the embassy, would you?"

Jordan raked his fingers through his too-long, dirty hair. "There isn't a need. If I can make it there, and let them do a fingerprint check, I can prove my identity. I may not have the opportunity if I'm wearing an enemy uniform." He didn't blame them for that reaction. He'd do the same thing in their position.

"But..." Adeela hesitated. "If you wear that uniform, walking out of here and around the city will be exponentially easier."

Putting his hands up in surrender, Jordan asked, "What do you want me to do?"

"Live. Any way you can," she replied. "And you can't if you stay here much longer or get shot on the way out."

She was right, Jordan realized. But that didn't help much. He watched the struggle play out on her face. "You have a solution?"

"Possible," she said.

"What?"

Adeela sat again. "How legal do you have to be?" His cocked eyebrow provided the encouragement she needed to describe the cargo truck stopping here en route to a plane going to the United States. The crew wouldn't ask questions if he didn't.

"I don't know..." Jordan rubbed his face. It went against everything the army trained him to do if he was ever taken prisoner by an enemy government. He wasn't supposed to talk to the people running the prison except about health or Geneva Convention cards, not give the opposing government any information—which he hadn't—and refuse favors. But then they were supposed to look for him for more than a day... And Nadar was supposed to be taking better care of him... No one was following the rules. "Okay," he said finally. "Only as a last resort."

Adeela smiled at him. "We'll get you home to Angel," she promised as she walked out.

Chapter Seventeen

OCTOBER 2013, BETHESDA, MARYLAND

"Troy, why don't the POWs know anything more than the American public?" Aaron asked when Troy came over to continue their research three weeks later.

"Hello to you too," Troy replied, stepping into the house. "Soldiers only know what they're told or what they see." He glanced around at the ransacked living room. "What's this?"

"I was looking for a newspaper article," Aaron replied. He'd had a lot of time to devote to the search since Keller had fired him for refusing to apologize to Colonel Bryant. Well, Keller cited the official reason as acting in a way unbecoming to a CIA officer. Whatever. He didn't need the money for a while, since he'd received Jordan's life insurance check. Of course, if he found Jordan alive, they would have to give the money back, but he'd rather figure that out with Jordan than not try. Unfortunately, the newspapers had run quite a few articles that caused the Americans to support the war effort for the first time in years.

Troy pushed some blankets to the opposite couch. "Aaron, I'm concerned about you."

"You and everyone else. I'm fine." Aaron typed on the computer. "Jordan, on the other hand, has been suffering for twenty-one days."

"I don't think he'd want you to suffer with him," Troy said.

"You don't understand. It's getting worse. He's hurting more." Aaron absently rubbed his back where he had seen Jordan getting whipped in his dreams last night. The guards had been ruthless—demanding answers Jordan still didn't have. The worst part was Aaron woke up consumed by Jordan's utter loss of hope.

"Even assuming he is alive, there's no way you have details—"

Red flashed before Aaron's eyes as his hands balled into fists.

Troy must have read his body language because he sighed and asked, "Will you come sit next to me, please?"

Aaron crossed the room in one stride. "Can't sit still. How about I get you something to eat?"

"So, you've been to the grocery store?"

"Yes. Like I said, I'm fine. Eating, drinking, even going outside once a day." *To get the mail.* "Now, listen, I called Doug Parks' wife..."

"You did what? We talked about this! You *cannot* give people false hope." Troy skidded his fingers through his hair. "What did you say?"

Aaron waved him off. "I asked how she was holding up. They've got three kids."

"*She* has three kids. Her husband is dead," Troy emphasized. "What else did you two discuss?"

"Um, the depths of my assholeness," Aaron told him. "She hasn't gotten over me missing the funeral." No one had, but he didn't expect them to understand.

Troy picked a piece of fuzz off Aaron's shirt. "All clean. And missing your spouse's funeral is kind of a difficult thing for people to get over. I was surprised his father respected your choice."

Aaron had gotten better at disguising his visceral reactions to Troy's insistent touching. Most of the time, the initiation of the touch was perfectly logical, but Troy always found reasons to linger longer than necessary. "Elliot and I have an understanding."

"Do you care that he has the flag?"

"No. I told him he could keep it." Aaron was grateful that Elliot made no claim to the life insurance money, because he needed that money to find Jordan.

"So, no luck on talking to the POWs or Captain Parks' wife. Have you found anything?"

Grabbing his computer, Aaron said, "Yes. I logged into my CIA account—"

"You were fired. Keller should have blocked you." Troy's eye twitched and Aaron again waved him off.

"*Okay*, so I hacked into the CIA website. I hadn't heard anything about the security guards they sent with Jordan and Doug. A few of them accused the same one of acting strange that day. Also, apparently, none of the POWs recognized him, but the papers all report the officers assisted in freeing the prisoners. You'd recognize your savior, no? Why isn't anyone looking into that?" Aaron bounced in his seat. But Troy did not match his excitement. His face had paled considerably as Aaron spoke. "Don't you think this means something?"

"Yes! It means you shouldn't be poking around where you don't belong. It means you could go to jail for accessing that." Troy took the computer from him and logged onto his email.

"No! It means there's a missing piece here. Someone who might know something..." Troy turned his computer back with a picture enlarged of a bloody, broken man. "What's that?"

"Jordan," Troy said. "I'm sorry."

All of Aaron's emotions seeped away as he scrutinized the picture. The man laid face-up with lashes on his chest and his head surrounded by blood. *No. This can't be Jordan... The almond eyes are all wrong and...* The ink on the man's arm caught Aaron's eye. "How long have you known?"

"I found out today."

"And you let me go on like that?" Aaron slammed the laptop shut.

"I didn't see any need for you to lose the hope you had been hanging onto."

Aaron shook his head. "The hope was a lie, Troy. All I ever wanted was the truth." But now that he had it, he understood even less. Not his heart or intuition. He didn't know who he was without that connection. "Leave."

Troy stroked his face. "You shouldn't be alone."

"I better get used to it," Aaron told him. "I'm fine." And he was. He didn't cry this time, but at least he could recognize it as denial now. Troy's touch failed to repulse him because he didn't feel that, either.

"Come with me, please. We'll get you some ice cream and watch chick flicks at my place."

The fact that Troy thought he could make decisions for him sparked a flame of rage in Aaron. "No! Get out. I need time."

"But..."

"Out!"

"Okay," Troy conceded. "I'll be around when you're ready."

AARON STUDIED THE photograph for the entire weekend, refusing to take Troy's calls. The man in the picture's wide almond eyes stared up at him as they had for forty-eight hours. Hollow. Empty. Not excited. Not optimistic. Certainly not happy.

Aaron's gaze traveled further down the body. Red lashes adorned the shoulders and chest. The dark skin was ashen. Chest still. He could not believe that the corpse in the photograph was his husband.

No. It wasn't. Jordan was passionate and loving, and everything Aaron had ever wanted. This picture was not him.

But...the grainy parachute on his inner arm confirmed to Aaron that it was Jordan's body. What pain had he endured to chase the life from his eyes? That, Aaron couldn't stomach contemplating. Why had Troy waited to show him? That pissed Aaron off on a whole other level. Rather, he was sure it would. Right then, Aaron couldn't muster anger. Or any other strong emotion. He set the picture down on the side table and pushed himself up. Aaron had a promise to keep.

Dressed in clean clothes after a hot shower, Aaron tucked the photograph into his back pocket and made his way to his car. He tried to sit, but couldn't get comfortable, as if the picture's jagged edges had the ability to cause real pain. So he removed it from his pocket and placed it on the center console. His hands shook as he inserted the key. His whole body pricked with anxiety. He glanced around. No one was in the street or hiding in the bushes. Why, then, did he feel like he was being watched?

Oh. Aaron acknowledged the wide almond eyes in the photograph with a nod and drove to his father-in-law's house. He got out and rang the doorbell.

When Elliot answered, Aaron forced a smile. "Can we talk, please?"

Elliot stepped aside. "As long as your words are more truthful than your expression."

Aaron pushed his still wet hair out of his face. "Always."

"Do you want tea?" Elliot asked.

"No, thank you." Aaron's hands were shaking too much to hold anything hot.

"Good, I don't like making tea anyway. Boiling water can cause too many problems and the little packets are difficult to maneuver," Elliot told him. "I'm sure you aren't here to debate the advantages of hot beverages."

"No, sir," Aaron answered.

"Are we back to that? You only call me 'sir' when you're afraid or nervous. Why would you be that? You're safe here."

"I know." Aaron fingered the photograph in his front pocket. He really should have rehearsed something. All his bravado had been washed down the shower drain. "I promised to tell you if I found anything concrete on Jordan."

"Ah." Elliot sat back. "Now, I understand. I guess it isn't happy news."

Aaron shook his head. "Troy gave me a...postmortem picture. Do you want to see it?"

"No, son. I'll take your word for it." After a pause, Elliot said, "Troy is the major general?"

"Yes," Aaron answered. Then met the elderly man's gaze. "Why?"

"I'm just surprised it was him who showed you."

Aaron blinked. "He knew I was looking."

"Aaron, the whole country knew you were searching. Every government agency has wished for you to stop the search. If any of them had the proof, they would have gladly offered it to you. How did the major general get the photograph?"

A flicker of hope flared, then died down. "I don't know, but it doesn't matter. It is Jordan."

Elliot heaved a sigh and appeared to be swallowing back emotions. "Do you feel better now that you know?"

"Honestly? I don't feel much of anything at the moment. But I wanted to be the one to tell you in case it shows up on the news or something."

"I appreciate that. You've always been a good man who made my son the happiest he's ever been," Elliot started.

Aaron slammed his eyes shut. He couldn't listen to his father-in-law rehash the joys of his marriage without breaking down. Aaron could not allow himself to think of never again hearing Jordan laugh, or call him Angel…

The photograph appeared behind his lids. Aaron shot up and ran to the bathroom where he vomited what little food he had eaten in the last few days. For the first time, the reality became clear. Try as he might to reject it, postpone it, or deny it, the hollow almond eyes of the man in the picture would never again light up with love and life. Aaron released a breath and flushed the toilet.

"I'm sorry," he said to Elliot when he emerged.

Elliot hugged him quickly. "You have nothing to apologize for. Remember, you have been my son since the day Jordan brought you home with the promise that he would be with you until he died. Nothing changes that." Aaron gave a short nod, but before he could turn away, Elliot touched his shoulder. "You did more than most would have in this situation. Don't for one second blame yourself. He loves you too much to want that."

Past tense now.

"That was present tense on purpose," Elliot responded to his unspoken thought. "You don't need a physical body to love. Remember that too."

"Thank you. I need to go home."

"Of course." Elliot stepped back. "Call me in a few days."

Aaron agreed and walked out of the door with legs of gelatin. He had no idea how he applied enough force to press the gas pedal, since he could not command that strength if he tried. For some reason, he wound up in front of Troy's house, as opposed to his own. Why? Wasn't he still angry? Yes. And he would tell Troy that. Aaron climbed out of the car and knocked on the door, which Troy answered in jeans and a Dora T-shirt.

"You should have told me earlier."

"You're right. I'm sorry." Troy replied. "Do you want to come in?"

Since nothing waited for him at home except silence—and he'd get enough of that over the coming years—Aaron said, "Nice shirt."

"Thanks. My daughter left a few minutes ago," Troy answered and stepped back to allow Aaron to enter.

"This doesn't change anything between us," Aaron told him.

"I understand. I'll wait," Troy promised.

Aaron knew without any doubt that Troy would be waiting a very long time, but he couldn't face the silence, so he walked in.

Chapter Eighteen

KABUL, AFGHANISTAN

The florescent bulb on top of Jordan's cell glowed for the...third...fourth day? He didn't know...anything, really. However long it had been since the guards had darkened his cell was the last time he'd slept...or ate. But then Jordan wasn't sure he could sleep if given the opportunity. His body throbbed from the beating the guards had delivered. He yearned to be able to sleep through them like he had the first one. All because he didn't fucking know where Jalalabad was or why he would be important to anyone other than the Muslim people. *If the US government has him, there's a reason. He's planning something, or...* Jordan couldn't think anymore. They kept threatening to kill him, which was possibly the worst part. What kind of people teased a man with relief, but never gave it to him? He hacked a deep cough, wiped the blood on his pillow, and flipped it over.

"That's getting worse," Adeela said from outside his cell.

"I guess," he responded. "Probably don't want to get too close."

Adeela opened the steel lock on the cell door and stepped in. "What did they do to you?"

Jordan shrugged and struggled off his concrete slab. "Usual. Restraints. Whips... I think. I can't turn my head far enough to see my back."

Adeela extended her hand to his shoulder but withdrew it. "May I?"

"I can't even bring myself to care." Jordan turned slightly so she could see his back.

"You have to care, Jordan. Why did they do this to you?"

Jordan tried to laugh, but it produced more blood than noise. "I don't ask why anymore. Too many whys. Why am I still here when I don't have the information they want? Why haven't they let me go? Or killed me?" His whole body shook. "I know. I know. I'm no good to them dead. Then, why haven't they called the US to say, 'What will you trade us for this useless person?'" Jordan's hacking coughs broke up his sobs. He was beyond the point of pride.

Adeela rubbed Jordan's shoulder. "They haven't killed you because it isn't your time to die. I won't accept it. Angel needs you."

"He thinks I'm dead too." Jordan closed his eyes at her gasp. He knew he couldn't hide it forever, but Jordan had assumed he'd make the choice to tell her rather than letting it slip.

"Angel is your wife, no?" Adeela asked.

"Husband," Jordan answered, and she simply stared at him. "Sorry. I couldn't risk people here finding out about my sexuality when I had any hope left."

"Well," she breathed, "that explains why you never expressed interest in me or the women on your base. Even the most loyal husband's gaze wanders after a few months without relief." Adeela removed alcohol swabs from her bag. "This may sting." She laughed softly at the incredulous look he shot her. "Yeah. You can handle it." After cleaning the welts silently for a moment, she asked, "Can you find a little bit of hope somewhere?"

"What's the point?"

"It's time for that last resort we discussed," Adeela stated, and Jordan's gaze shot up. "You can be on American soil in forty-eight hours."

"Why? How?" Jordan's mind cleared ever so slightly.

"I told you, it isn't your time to go. You have to do everything you can so Angel gets his husband back."

Jordan kept eye contact with her over his shoulder. "They had enough toying with me? Realized I knew nothing and are ready to kill me?"

"No, someone from your military, um, found out that you were alive...and was outraged that Anwar had not killed you," Adeela explained. "I got the sense from what I heard of the conversation that they'd spoken before."

Jordan swallowed the bile threatening to emerge. "Military? Who? What's their rank? Do you know?"

"They were high up and working for another government agency. I only heard bits and pieces of Anwar's conversation with him and Obaid."

"Adeela, this is so important. What agency? FBI? DoD? White House?" Jordan guessed, his heart racing.

"No, this is *not* important. You have to move so you can escape. Tonight," she countered.

"It *is* important. If the wrong people want me dead, I don't have anywhere to escape *to*. So, I might as well let your government kill me. Please try to remember his ranking. Name. Agency. *Anything*," Jordan begged.

"Person. Not people. I did not get the impression he alerted anyone else. C—"

"CIA?"

"Yes, that's right!"

"The man they spoke to was a high-ranking military official in the CIA?" At her nod, Jordan fisted a stone on the ground and threw it at the bars. "Fucking Hart!"

Adeela grabbed his wrists. "Are you crazy? There are guards outside."

"Sorry. How can I escape?" *I have a major general to kill.* The adrenaline blocked out Jordan's pain as he listened to Adeela describe when the cargo truck would stop in front of the prison before heading to a plane to Bethesda, Maryland. The crew wouldn't ask questions if he didn't.

She handed him an Afghanistan army uniform. "Put it on."

He inspected the jungle camo. Jordan had no more options. "Come with me," he said as he dressed in the uniform.

"So that I can be stoned to death for adultery? No, thank you," Adeela replied. "The men taking you home would turn us both over to the local authorities. And the beheading Anwar has planned for you tomorrow will look like fun compared to how we're killed."

Jordan rubbed his neck. Again, Adeela was right. *Damn it.* "All right. When I get home, I'll send for you."

"Anwar won't—"

"Be around to comment once I tell the government the story." *Neither will Hart if I have anything to say about it.*

Adeela stroked his cheek. "Angel's a lucky man. Get yourself home safely."

"Will you come to America when I find a way?"

"Yes, but worry about your life first." She helped him stand and handed him a walking stick to support his ankle.

"Thank you, Adeela." Jordan caught her gaze. For the first time since he'd met her, she shied away. "I owe you everything."

"No, nothing," she answered. "I'm happy to help."

Jordan hobbled to the unlocked cell door. "Hey, how are you avoiding trouble?"

Adeela gave him a wry smile. "You stabbed me while I was cleaning your wounds."

"Sorry," he said between coughs, which had increased since he'd stood.

She shook her head. "Go. And use the gun in your food bag to shoot anyone who stops you. Leave before Anwar comes looking for me."

Jordan sent a prayer of thanks, sadness, and hope for them all as he hobbled out of the building into the night air.

JORDAN SHIVERED ON the bench of the rickety, pitch-black cargo truck on the way to the plane that would take him, the two-man crew, and whatever they were carrying to Maryland at around midnight on Sunday. On a commercial jet, a flight from most parts of Afghanistan would take about seven or eight hours. The tiny plane, however, would need to stop twice for fuel, once in Egypt and once in Liberia. So, the importers—as Jordan liked to think of them—had a thirty-hour trip planned once the plane left the ground. But, first, they had to get there. The truck swayed as it ascended the mountain, sending a heavy wooden box across the floor. He used all his strength in an attempt to brace it with his healthy leg, but the box crashed against his injured ankle. Jordan stuffed his fist in his mouth to stifle the scream. The importers would not appreciate a noisy unnamed loader. They knew him only as Adeela's friend. And that was enough to get him home.

But then again...home to what? Aaron thought he was dead. What if he'd moved on to another man? Jordan shuddered at the thought he had put out of his mind for a month. Of course, Aaron had every right to see other people after Jordan's death. That didn't mean Jordan couldn't hold out hope that he hadn't fallen for someone else. Jordan coughed into his shirtsleeve, quickly wiping his mouth of the blood. He had to believe that Angel would welcome him home if he was going to push through the next day and a half.

He could not even begin to think of his job at the moment. Jordan had no plans for how he would convince the US government that one of their own had attempted to have him killed. *Maybe my captors lied. No. Well, some of them might have, but not Adeela. I hope. No!* She hadn't lied. The people above her had to have given her bad information. That was the only possibility Jordan could live with. Literally. Because if she lied about anything, he'd be killed within hours by the importers, their friends, or a foreign government.

Jordan slammed his head against the truck wall as the brakes screeched to a halt. He tried his best to catch the blood dripping down the back of his skull and neck with one of the clean shirts Adeela had put in his bag.

The steel door cranked open, revealing the driver with his arms crossed, chewing his tobacco. The clouds hung heavy and gray. "Looking for an engraved invitation, boy? Get your ass up and put these boxes in the plane."

Jordan limped off the truck with the help of his makeshift walking stick. Ten boxes, about a hundred pounds apiece, needed to be transferred. As he stared at them, trying to construct a plan, the driver kicked his stick hard enough to snap it in half.

"I need that!" Jordan cried out and grabbed onto the side of the truck.

"Can't carry boxes with a stick. Adeela promised you'd be useful. Earn ya keep or I leave ya here." The driver spat on the ground and went with the other crew member to talk to the pilot.

Tossing his meager belongings on top of one of the boxes, Jordan leaned as much of his weight on his uninjured leg as he could manage and carried the box the ten feet to the plane. Tears stung his eyes as the desert sand burned his feet through the holes in his shoes. *One down, nine more to go.*

"Excuse me," the other crew member said, approaching Jordan. "Do you speak English?"

"Yes," Jordan responded. This man spoke to him with respect. Why?

"Read it?" he asked. Jordan nodded. "The map they gave us is written in English. We can't understand it. If you read the map, I will unload the boxes."

"Thank you," Jordan said, though that man likely wasn't doing him any favors. He hobbled over to the man standing with the driver. "Are you the pilot?"

"Yes, and that stupid man gave me an American map. It's probably labeled wrong too." The pilot went on to bitch about stupid Americans not knowing anything but what's in front of them. "You read stupid language?"

"Yes," Jordan answered, and the man thrust the map into his hand. He blinked at it, waiting for the language to make sense again after using Farsi for the past...three months? How much time had passed? He'd stopped keeping track.

"Well...? Do you understand or no?"

"I can get you where you need to go."

"Why should I trust a convict?"

Do you have a choice? "I was a prisoner, not a convict. Your other option is to wait around and hope someone else in this town knows English." Jordan probably should have been more careful with his words, since he depended on this man to get him home.

The pilot narrowed his eyes to scrutinize Jordan, who couldn't bring himself to care what judgments he made. "What'd you do?"

"What are you carrying?" Jordan threw back.

The pilot nodded. "Don't ask, don't tell. You read. Get us where it says. You can live."

Never thought I'd appreciate don't ask, don't tell. "We'll get there," he promised, more for himself than the pilot. Had he not been in pain and exhausted, Jordan would have offered to fly, but even he knew that was beyond his capabilities. On the plane, the other crew member arranged the boxes. "Need help?"

"Need to get done. Faster if I do it alone," he replied. "Long as we get to Maryland before dawn on Sunday, I'm happy with you reading the map."

Ah, so there's a time limit. Jordan was just as happy not to put too much pressure on his foot. He took a slug of his water bottle in an attempt to limit the deep cough, but it only fueled the blood and mucus from his lungs onto his arm.

"Hey, we don't deal with dead bodies," the guy in the back warned.

"I'm fine," Jordan answered.

"Your shirt disagrees. What's wrong with you?"

Jordan shook his head. "I need to get home and find out."

BY THE TIME the cargo plane touched down at twelve thirty Sunday morning, Jordan still did not know the names of his flying companions or what they carried. But he cared even less and bid them goodbye before he had to find out. Jordan limped to the nearest corner and glanced around. He needed to get home...without money, a car, or clean clothes. Not to mention no food or water. The hunger pains had been constant for the last day. He blinked at the street sign. And assessed he was a mile from home.

I can do this, he chanted silently. *I've come this far. One more mile to warmth, and Angel...hopefully.* Jordan could not entertain any other possibilities, or else he'd never make it. He considered stopping at a police station for help, but what would he say? "I'm Jordan Collins. You can find my name listed under military causalities, but I'm actually alive. Please call my husband?" No, that would require too much explanation. Jordan pulled his injured leg with him, slowing his pace considerably, but what else could he do? *Nothing. Keep walking.*

Chapter Nineteen

OCTOBER 2013, BETHESDA, MARYLAND

"Well, that was as lame as the first few times I've seen it," Aaron told Troy on the way out of a midnight showing of *The Rocky Horror Picture Show* the weekend before Halloween.

"Of course, it's lame! That's the point. I told you it would be more fun if you dressed the part."

"Dressing in drag is beyond what I've budgeted for fun," Aaron said, tightening his jacket against the assault of the cold fall air. On the other hand, Troy had no issue wearing women's lingerie, fishnet stockings, and high-heeled shoes. Not to mention inch-thick makeup. "So... I'll talk to you tomorrow." *Or something.*

Troy stopped Aaron from turning around with a hand to his shoulder. "What are we doing?"

"Going home to sleep. It's way past my bedtime. Probably past yours too." If Aaron took the right amount of Ambien and watched enough TV, what he said might actually be true.

"No, I mean, us, what are *we* doing?" At Aaron's blank stare, Troy threw his hands up. "Jesus, Aaron, I believed in you when everyone else thought you were crazy. I helped you find the truth about Jordan. I've tried to be patient and understanding of your process, but every time I think we're getting closer, you push me away again."

Aaron blinked and shook his head. "What do you want from me, Troy? Commitment? Love? I can't."

"Yet." Troy stepped closer. "You've come further than you realize."

My acting skills must be better than I gave myself credit for.

"To answer your question, I want you. You need to let me in if we're going to continue dating, even if it's only a little."

Aaron swallowed the bile that rose in his throat at the term dating. He wasn't dating Troy. Aaron wasn't dating *anybody.* He'd married Jordan with the intention of never dating again.

"Listen, I know I'll never be Jordan. I get it. But—" Troy paused to touch Aaron's cheek. "—could you be my angel?"

Aaron pushed him away. "Don't you *ever* call me that." He ran his hands through his thinning blond hair as he studied Troy. The man had supported him as much as anyone could over the last few months. Gotten him out of the house, reminded him to eat, and helped make the connection that landed him a telecommuting IT job. Aaron might not be functioning at all had it not been for Troy. He deserved some reward for all he'd done. "Follow me home, but understand, I'm not promising anything."

"Yes, sir," Troy replied with a goofy grin.

Aaron hoped he hadn't seen him roll his eyes as they got in their separate cars. On second thought, nope. He didn't care if he had.

HE FLIPPED ON the light twenty minutes later and led Troy into the living room. Troy's expectations thickened the air to the point that Aaron almost felt the need to clear it with his hands before walking. *Could I be more melodramatic?* "You can wash your face."

"Don't want lipstick on you?" Troy teased.

Don't want you *on me.* Aaron shook his head and pointed Troy toward the bathroom as he sank down on the couch. The expectations were reasonable if he and Troy were dating. He shuddered at the idea. *Don't both people have to agree upon that? Have I been out of the dating world so long that now it's just assumed?* Aaron stiffened as Troy wrapped his arms around him from behind. "You move quietly."

"Military taught me well."

Aaron lost any response he may have had when Troy planted a kiss to his neck. And then another. "Troy, no. I can't." His stomach flipped and his hair stood on end. Everything about the contact felt wrong.

"You can, Angel. Relax." Troy tightened his hold on Aaron and moving his lips up to Aaron's face.

"I told you never to call me that," Aaron growled. "Let go of me." *Why did I sit down?* Aaron's greatest advantage was his height, and now it was lost.

"Come on," Troy started, but stumbling footsteps drew Aaron's attention outside.

"Shh!" Aaron pushed him away with a surge of adrenaline. "Do you hear that?"

"What?"

"There's someone outside."

Troy shook his head. "I don't hear anything."

The footsteps crunched the fallen leaves. A shadow moved past the living room window. Aaron stood. "I saw someone."

"They're passing by. Let's get back to what we were doing." Troy tugged on his arm.

We weren't doing anything. But in light of an intruder, the sentiment was not worth addressing. *Maybe the person wouldn't even approach the house. Maybe...fuck!* The intruder moved the wall-mounted thermometer where Aaron hid his extra key.

"Aaron, honey, it's nothing," Troy tried.

"It's not only something; it's someone who knows where I keep the key to the kitchen door," Aaron told him, slipping his feet into shoes and formulating a plan. *Slide flat against the wall, grab gun, aim at intruder.* Burglars avoided confrontation. *I can do this.*

The kitchen lock turned. "Shit. I'll call the cops."

"No. I'm going to handle it." Aaron's voice and nerves calmed for no discernible reason. Someone was entering his house uninvited. Yet, his pulse slowed, and his thoughts had a logical progression again.

"What? You can't go out there alone."

Aaron pressed his finger to his lips and directed, "Be quiet. No phone calls."

"You could be killed."

"I know how to defend myself. Enough, Troy." Aaron edged out of the living room. He sucked in a breath, his gaze fixed on the shadowy figure struggling with the lock. *Are they drunk?* Aaron wondered as he extracted the Glock 17 from the hall table and pressed it to his body. The man wore no jacket in the October night.

"Aaron!" Troy called from the living room.

"Shut up!" he responded. "I will know when and if it's time to panic. It's not."

"Your instincts have been wrong before. You'll get yourself killed," Troy protested further. "I'm calling the cops."

"Not yet." Aaron had nothing to account for his confidence. The only other person who knew where they kept that key was dead, which meant the one coming in had to be a stalker. Finally, a coughing man stumbled in the door and slapped the wall. Aaron advanced through the shadows while Troy's eyes burned into the back of his head. As the overhead light illuminated the room, Aaron dashed from the darkened hall into the kitchen.

The man hunched over, groping for something, his eyes squeezed tight, as if afraid of the light. He coughed harder and dragged his right foot with every step he took. Then slid down the wall.

"Freeze or I'll shoot!" Aaron yelled and aimed the gun at his chest.

"Angel, no, please." Hacking fluid-filled coughs broke up the intruder's words.

Angel. Angel. Angel. The term of endearment reverberated through Aaron's heart. "Jordan?" Aaron whispered.

"Yes." He coughed red into his dirty hand. "Please help."

Impossible! Jordan had been executed in Afghanistan. He'd seen the picture. "No! Jordan's dead." Aaron's hand shook so hard his grip on the gun loosened.

The person on the floor lifted his warm brown almond-shaped eyes to meet Aaron's and sputtered, "Not unless you shoot." Despite his words being broken and laden with whatever he was coughing up, Jordan spoke without fear, as though he didn't have a gun pointed in his face.

Aaron set the Glock on the table. He held it down while keeping his eyes locked on Jordan's. Not moving closer. "How?"

Before Jordan could answer, the front door shut. Aaron and Jordan jolted as Troy skittered along the sidewalk in his bright red heels. *Fucking coward.* Aaron would have to deal with that particular mess later. And it was becoming more of a mess by the damn second.

"Who was that?" Jordan asked, struggling to sit straighter, his gaze darting around the room.

"Um." Aaron glanced at the door and back again. "Troy."

Jordan's eyes widened in apparent fear as his breath came in short spurts, increasing his coughing...and the blood on his sleeve.

Aaron crouched in front of Jordan and focused on the physical ailments. "You need to go to the hospital."

"Not yet." He coughed again. "Are you seeing him?"

"No. He's my only friend right now." At Jordan's confused expression, Aaron explained, "When they told me you died, I lost it because their story sucked. Cost me my job. Troy stuck by me and helped me investigate your 'death.'" Aaron put air quotes around the last word. "Then he..."

"He what?" Jordan prompted.

"Showed me a picture of your body after they executed you. But...you obviously weren't dead."

"No."

Aaron's mind swam from the onslaught of information and emotions. "Troy must have made a mistake." The words were hollow, but they were the only ones that made sense of his life.

"You don't believe that."

Aaron shook his head. "Why were you scared when I told you his name?"

"He kept me there on purpose," Jordan sputtered.

"Jor—"

His head snapped up and he caught Aaron's gaze. "Don't give me that condescending tone." More coughing.

"I'm sorry," Aaron whispered. "I just..."

"Angel." Jordan softened his voice. "I can't tell you how I know yet, but I promise you, I do."

Aaron hesitated only slightly before saying, "I believe you." And he did. He believed Jordan more than any story the officers or Troy had told him over the last couple of months.

"Thank you." Jordan extended his hand and brushed Aaron's cheek. "My Angel."

That simple touch broke the dam. Aaron's tears streaked a line through the dirt Jordan had painted on his face. "Oh, Jordan," Aaron cried, kissing his palm, igniting his husband's own wet cheeks. "'I love you' is not strong enough."

Jordan leaned forward and kissed Aaron's cheeks. "Maybe not, but we are. If..."

"If what?"

"If you still want to be." Jordan flitted his gaze away again.

"Yes, more than you know," Aaron answered. "Let's get to the hospital."

He shook his head. "I can't."

Aaron scrutinized him. "You're coughing blood and as pale as I've ever seen you."

"I have either TB or pneumonia, an ankle that's been broken repeatedly, and I haven't slept in at least three days," Jordan reported between coughs.

"Um. Yeah. You need a doctor. Probably a team of doctors." Aaron started to stand up, but Jordan grabbed his arm.

"The army thinks I'm dead."

"Uh-huh. We're not making them prophetic." Aaron extracted his phone from his pocket. As he dialed the last number, Jordan snatched the phone and threw it across the kitchen. "Jordan!"

"I can't! Angel, what if they court-martial me?"

"They fucked up, not you. Why would you be in trouble?"

"Adeela helped me escape. Not supposed to accept help from the enemy..." Jordan gestured to the torn material on his legs. "Afghanistan army uniform pants." Before Aaron could process the words, he added, "I didn't work for them or give them information."

"I never questioned. Do the pants have the GPS tracking like your uniforms?"

"I don't know. I should have asked..." Jordan hyperventilated.

Aaron placed what he hoped was a calming hand on one of Jordan's. "Take them off. We'll put them in the trash compactor. Unless you want to give them to Bryant."

"I don't know. I...don't know anything right now." Jordan wrapped his arms across his chest and exerted effort to steady his erratic breathing.

Aaron cupped Jordan's chin with his other hand. "I know something. My husband overcame every obstacle to get home to me. I don't care how."

"They might."

"Your job as a POW is to make it home alive, without betraying the interests of the United States. You did that. I will not let the effort go to waste," Aaron told him. "We're getting you help."

"Stay with me?" Jordan begged.

"Every minute you aren't in surgery or telling the officers about your heroic escape," Aaron replied with a kiss.

Jordan hesitated for a long moment and nodded on his exhale. Aaron called the ambulance and put them on speakerphone. The 911 operator moved much faster when he dropped the words "tuberculosis" and "Afghanistan."

"On their way," Aaron told Jordan as he hung up.

Jordan gave another nod. "Angel, did you have to pick Hart to lean on?"

"I'm sorry. I didn't have many options. And I thought he could help find you."

"I understand." Jordan might have added more, but the paramedics banged on the door. It would have to wait.

Chapter Twenty

AARON KISSED JORDAN goodbye as he watched the doctors wheel him into surgery. No. Not goodbye. That implied permanence. The doctors were only setting a broken ankle. People lived through those surgeries all the time. Jordan had survived more than a month in an Afghanistan prison. Aaron couldn't even account for how Jordan made it home that didn't involve superpowers. Who knows what he'd caught there and during his escape? What if the doctors found an infection and had to cut off his foot? Or ruptured an artery? He could bleed out. Die on an operating table.

The thought almost propelled Aaron through the double doors into the operating room. Instead, he sank down with his head between his knees. *Wait.* Jordan had enough superpowers to live through all of that. A simple surgery would not bring him down. Jordan was his hero. *No. Not was. Is. Jordan is my hero.*

"Excuse me," a woman said.

Aaron lifted his face to find the triage nurse standing above him.

"Are you all right?"

"Physically, yes."

She offered a smile. "I imagine your head's pretty messed up right now."

"Understatement." He laughed a little. The nurse had been the one to admit them, so she had heard the story of the army thinking Jordan was dead. But clearly, Jordan was not dead. However, he had been locked in an Afghanistan prison since September and could have pneumonia or tuberculosis, in addition to his broken ankle. They ran that test before the words even left his mouth. Tuberculosis would have landed Jordan in isolation, the mention of which sent him into a panic. Not that Aaron blamed him. Come to think of it, he likely would not allow it either. How would he prevent the hospital from forcing Jordan into isolation? Thankfully, the tests came back showing a clear indication of bacterial pneumonia.

"Is there anyone you should call?"

Aaron blinked. "Call? You mean his commanding officers? I thought the hospital already did." Which was a good thing. The high military officers wanted to deal with Aaron even less than he wanted to deal with them. Colonel Bryant would board a flight from Chicago that would arrive in the DC airport sometime tomorrow.

"I meant family. Is there anyone you don't want to find out about Jordan's return on the news?"

Aaron's eyes popped open. "Oh, God, yes. I should call his father."

The nursed laughed. "I'd recommend it."

"Thanks." Aaron took out his phone. Six a.m. Elliot would most likely be asleep. *Better that way. He'll have had no time to watch the morning news.* "What am I supposed to say? 'Hey, your only son who you thought was dead is actually not'? His father isn't young. The shock could kill him."

She patted Aaron's arm with a wrinkled hand and stood. "Don't underestimate people who 'aren't young.'"

"Yes, ma'am," Aaron replied with a blush. He stretched and made his way out the door. Aaron's thumb quivered above the green phone icon. Jordan's return was fantastic news, but difficult to explain when Aaron didn't have all the information. He pressed the button and listened to the shrill rings.

"Hello," Elliot answered groggily.

"Hi, Elliot, it's Aaron. I'm sorry to wake you."

"Aaron? What's wrong?" Elliot asked, sounding more alert now.

"Um, nothing's wrong...exactly." *I should have thought this out better.* "I'm at Walter Reed. Can you please come?" *Who's chicken shit? Yeah, baby, that would be me.*

Silence. "Nothing's wrong, but you want me to come to the army hospital?" Elliot's words were slow, giving Aaron plenty of time to think about the ridiculousness of the request.

"Please?"

"They always did have the best coffee. I'll leave now."

"Thank you." Aaron ended the call and checked the time. Jordan's surgery would last another three hours. And it would take Elliot twenty minutes to get there. Plenty of time to walk around the block. His phone beeped. Second text from Troy. *Answering him would be a terrible idea seeing as I have no idea what to say to him either. If what Jordan told me is true... No.* Aaron would not play that game. He had to believe his husband, which meant he had to hate Troy. And he did. All Aaron wanted was for something in his life to make sense.

"Aaron!" Elliot called as Aaron rounded the corner to reach the front of the hospital again.

"Good morning." Aaron jogged over to offer Elliot an arm, for which he received a scowl.

"Thank you, but no. I can walk, not as fast as you, but my cane and I get there just fine. Why are you running?" Elliot asked as they approached the hospital.

"I...had some energy to release." He transferred his weight from foot to foot and did not meet his father-in-law's eyes.

Elliot touched his shoulder. "There's no need to be nervous. I know why you called me here."

Squinting, Aaron asked, "You do?"

"Yes, son. While I appreciate it, a few hours won't change much."

A few hours changed everything. A few hours ago, Aaron was convinced he was a widower, and now Jordan was getting his broken ankle fixed. "Why do you think I asked you to come?"

"Because the army sent home Jordan's body for a proper burial," Elliot answered, and Aaron shook his head. "Then why Walter Reed, the army hospital?"

Aaron averted his gaze. "I think we better go inside and get one of those coffees. You should sit down." Despite looking like he wanted to argue, Elliot followed Aaron into the hospital and down to the cafeteria, where Aaron bought them both black coffees. He handed it to his father-in-law and said, "Jordan is in surgery."

"Organ donation?" Elliot stared at Aaron when he shook his head again.

"To fix his broken ankle," Aaron whispered in reply.

"Why fix a broken ankle he won't ever walk on? Isn't there a better use of resources?" Elliot's voice heightened in fear and confusion.

Aaron gave him a smile that was probably much less reassuring than he hoped. "You wouldn't even accept my arm to help you inside. I don't think telling your son he won't ever walk again is a great idea."

"Aaron, that is not funny."

"No, it's not. He likes walking."

have a visitor," he announced, admitting Aaron and hurrying away.

"Hey, you." Aaron walked over and kissed him. His lips lingered on Jordan's skin a moment, appreciating the heat and cushion he never thought he'd feel again. "How are you feeling?"

"High," Jordan answered. "Like my foot."

"What?"

Jordan pointed to his suspended leg. "My foot is high."

Aaron laughed. "We're gonna keep you on the ground for now."

"But I wanna fly." Jordan's whine turned to a cough.

Aaron kissed his head and wiped his mouth with a tissue. "No jumping out of airplanes for a while."

"I'll wait a few weeks. Doctor said this'll be on for at least five." Jordan leaned his head on Aaron's hip, because that was where the bed was positioned. "Would you sit down so they don't think we're being inappropriate?"

"You're fun when you're high." Aaron perched on the edge of the bed and wrapped an arm around his husband. "Listen, your dad's here."

Jordan's eyes widened. "What was his reaction? He thought I was dead too, right?"

"Yes, he did. He's...concerned and not entirely sure he should believe it, which I get, because I'm not always sure if I do," Aaron explained. "Are you up to seeing him?"

"He's going to be angry," Jordan replied after a few beats.

"At...? The government? The army? Troy? Yes, to all."

"No, at me. For accepting favors."

"The very thought that anyone will be angry at you makes my blood boil in ways you cannot even imagine." Aaron calmed his breathing. "I promise your dad is not blaming you. He's confused, but he thought he was coming here to collect your remains for burial. Ankle surgery and pneumonia are a much better outcome."

"Please stay while he's here, just in case you're wrong."

Aaron planted another kiss to his forehead. "I will, but I'm not wrong. I'll be right back."

He left Jordan's area and found Elliot wearing the required gown, mask, and gloves. "Hey, I know this isn't an issue, but Jordan is afraid you're angry at him."

"Why in the world would he think that?" Elliot asked.

"Because he didn't follow all the rules about the proper way to get home, and... Elliot, where are you going?" Aaron grasped his arm not supporting the cane.

"To tell my son he is ridiculous."

"That may not be the best way to go."

"I know how to speak to my son."

Aaron inhaled sharply. "But without my okay, you won't be able to. He needs our support. He'll have plenty of people questioning his decisions."

Elliot stared at Aaron for a long moment. "Of course, I will be supportive. Please take me to him."

Aaron nodded and led him to Jordan's curtained-off area.

Jordan opened his eyes and squeaked, "Hi, Dad."

As he glanced from Jordan to Aaron, Elliot's cane wobbled.

"Sit, please." Aaron offered him the chair by Jordan's bed.

Taking the seat, Elliot blinked several times and finally shook his head. "I was going to ask how you made it home alive, but I don't care." The elderly man, who'd remained stoic throughout the last two months, allowed his voice to betray the relief which turned to anger with his next words. "We will bring Hart down. He will pay for this."

"Dad." Jordan placed his wired hand on top of Elliot's arm. "We can't tell anyone. Not yet. No one will believe me now."

"Jordan, he..."

"Did things I can't describe here without proof."

"Where do I get the proof? I want him behind bars."

Aaron advanced toward them and placed a hand on Elliot's shoulder. The desperate tone in his voice correlated too closely with Jordan's rapid breathing. "So do we, but we have to respect Jordan's wishes."

"What if he comes after him?" Elliot questioned, fear playing out on his face.

"Then you can join the people who will kill him." Aaron spoke in a low tone and squeezed Jordan's hand. "No one is going to hurt Jordan."

Chapter Twenty-One

"CAPTAIN, I'M SORRY," Colonel Bryant said at the hospital the next morning after Jordan related the story of his escape from the Afghanistan prison two days ago. "Our sources were all sure you had died. Otherwise, we would have continued looking for you."

"I believe you, sir. No hard feelings," Jordan replied. He had no animosity toward Bryant, because Bryant had every reason to think the fire killed Jordan along with the Afghan prisoners and Lieutenant Parks. The only person Jordan blamed was Hart, but he could not share that information yet. Bryant wouldn't appreciate it without a lot of proof.

"What I don't understand is how you knew you were going to be executed..."

"Yesterday," Jordan finished Bryant's train of thought. "I told you, I overheard the guards discussing a phone call between Nadar and a United States official. When the person refused to negotiate, the enemy decided I wasn't worth keeping alive. So, they set my execution for dawn." Yes, Jordan had thought many times about the fact that if he had not escaped when he did, he wouldn't be alive right now. The frantic conversation came flooding back...

Jordan shook his head to stop the flashback. To protect himself and Adeela, he changed the story to say he'd overheard the guards talking about their plans. All he had told Bryant about her was that she had taken care of him in the prison and had "accidentally" dropped a piece of paper with information about a cargo plane to the United States in his cell weeks before. He then explained he'd hitched a ride on a delivery truck and offered to read the English map to the US for the pilot in exchange for a ride home. And he went with the marginally more credible statement that the US official refused to negotiate. Jordan hoped the suggestion of a phone call ordering his execution would propel the government into an investigation where they would find the truth themselves.

"Surely, you don't believe that someone in our government would treat your life so flippantly."

Jordan bit his lip. Technically, Hart worked for the government. "No, sir, I only know what I overheard."

"They were wrong."

No. They weren't. Jordan took a jagged breath. "Please look into it. I'm not making this up."

"I never accused you of any such thing. I said the guards were wrong. But we will investigate."

"And Adeela? Will you help her?"

"Captain," Colonel Bryant began, "I'm grateful you made it out. But—"

"But he shouldn't have been able to," Dr. Jacklyn, the internist assigned to Jordan's case, said, entering the room. "He's a strong one, Colonel. I've never seen someone survive with pneumonia that bad, much less walk a mile on a badly broken ankle."

"Our Captain Collins is a hardy one. Always has been," Bryant replied. "He'll be all right?"

The doctor smiled. "I see no reason why not, as long as he supports that ankle and takes his antibiotics. We're only keeping him one more day for observation because he has someone at home to take care of him."

"Do you think your husband can handle that?" Bryant questioned. "If not, the army will pay for an in-home nurse."

Jordan cringed. "Yes, I'm sure he can." Not that he was, but Bryant didn't need to know that. Aaron left for the first time when Bryant arrived to talk to him. He sent up a quick prayer that Aaron would return. They had promised to stick together, but a small part of Jordan feared it would be too much for Aaron. He'd read the home care instructions and would be on his back for a while. Jordan vowed to learn to use crutches as quickly as possible so as not to be a burden.

"If that changes, you have a number to call," Bryant reminded him.

Taking his cringe as a sign of pain, Dr. Jacklyn handed Jordan the morphine pump. "Press that button if you need some relief." To Bryant, she said, "He needs to rest. I think whatever you have to discuss with him can wait a few days or weeks."

"Of course. We just have to come up with a plan to address the media, should he encounter any reporters on his way out of the hospital," Bryant replied.

Dr. Jacklyn nodded. "You have five minutes."

"He can't have visitors after five minutes? You may want to tell Aaron. He's the tall blond man in the waiting room. You can't miss him," Colonel Bryant told her, making Jordan's heart skip a beat.

"I know who Aaron is. And no, I don't have to tell him anything. I asked you to leave in five minutes because Jordan doesn't need stress. I will not have you driving up my patient's blood pressure, Colonel." The doctor patted Jordan's shoulder and added to Bryant before leaving, "You now have three minutes."

"Yes, Doctor," Bryant replied and turned to Jordan. "Captain, I don't want you to get in trouble for making friends over there. If the wrong people hear about you asking the US government to help an enemy's wife, it could turn out very badly. I will explore the supposed phone call to the Afghan leaders. But from here on out you tell people that you got a ride from some rich Americans."

"That doesn't make sense," Jordan protested.

"It will," Bryant answered. "Captain Collins, I'm looking out for you here. Keep it quiet. That's an order." With that, Bryant strode out of the room and shut the door.

But Jordan didn't hear the wood door meeting the frame. Instead, heavy metal bars slammed together. A key turned, stealing the heat from the room, the softness of the bed, and the air from his lungs. His chest tightened as men outside his cell screamed in Farsi. *Fine. Yell from out there. Don't come in. Please don't come in.* But...the silent pleas worked no better now than they ever did.

"I don't know anything! Stop!" Jordan tried to scream. He threw the gag covering his mouth across the room. Though it would do no good, Jordan threw punches into the air when one of them called for restraints. *Not this time, you bastards!*

AARON RUSHED IN with the doctors and nurses when the red light outside Jordan's room started flashing red and beeping, signaling a dangerous change in his vitals. "What happened?" Aaron demanded of Dr. Jacklyn.

"I don't know. Stay back," she ordered as Jordan thrashed about on the bed, shaking the material suspending his leg. "We need restraints. He's going to hurt himself."

"Restraints? You can't be serious." Aaron stepped up to the bed and glanced from Jordan to the doctor. Anguish distorted his husband's expression. "He just spent several weeks in a prison enduring who knows what kind of torture."

"He's endangering himself, Aaron. Step away or I'll force you to leave." The doctor reached for the restraints an orderly handed her.

Aaron wrapped his arms around Jordan and leaned onto his chest. "Jordan, you're safe. No one's going to hurt you anymore."

"Let go of him." The male orderly grabbed Aaron's shoulder.

Aaron shook the man off. "The nightmare's all over now," Aaron soothed against Jordan's ear.

Behind him, the doctor murmured about Jordan's vitals stabilizing. The shaking died down. And after a few minutes, Jordan returned Aaron's embrace. "Oh, Angel, they got you too. I'm sorry. I never wanted to drag you here." The yelling had turned to sobbing. "I'm sorry. You don't deserve this."

Here? "Open your eyes, love. We're both safe." Aaron eased up on Jordan so he could look around.

"I'm in the States?" Jordan wiped his face.

"Yeah," Aaron answered. "Do you remember getting here?" The medical professionals scurried around them reading machines and taking notes, but Aaron kept his face close to Jordan's so as not to overwhelm him.

"Plane and walking, and, fuck, this hurts," Jordan responded. "God, I was there again. So cold."

"Flashbacks are a normal part of PTSD," Dr. Jacklyn told them. "Aaron knew how to handle it. Next time, we'll listen to your instincts."

Well, wouldn't that have saved us a whole lot of trouble? "Would you please pass the suggestion on to Colonel Bryant?"

"I don't think that would be well-received. Sorry. I'll make a note to avoid restraints," Dr. Jacklyn added. "Did Jordan tell you they were a problem for him?"

"No." Aaron held Jordan's hand. "I just...knew."

She gestured everyone else out of the room. "You let me know if you need anything else."

"Thanks."

As Dr. Jacklyn went to shut the door, Jordan called, "Wait. Please don't. I think that's what triggered it."

Once she'd walked out, leaving the door cracked, Aaron kissed Jordan's hand. "So, no closed doors?"

"Not inside. Sorry." Jordan cast his gaze to the bed.

Aaron lifted his chin and searched his face for the confident husband he knew. *He's there. He'll come out when he feels safe again.* "Why are you sorry? Now, I don't have to break the habit of leaving the bathroom door open. I did that while you were away."

"Well, we won't have to worry about that anymore." Jordan nuzzled against Aaron's chest.

"I am so glad." Aaron kissed his head.

"That I don't have to go away again?"

"No! That I don't have to pretend to have manners all the time. It's exhausting, you know."

Jordan's chuckle turned to a cough. He pulled away from Aaron just long enough to finish and lay back down again. "Thank you, Angel," he whispered.

Aaron held him tightly while he fell into a relaxed slumber. *We can probably take bondage off things to play with in the bedroom too*, Aaron thought as he stroked his sleeping husband.

His phone beeped with another text from Troy.

We need to talk.

Aaron deleted it. Never again.

Chapter Twenty-Two

BANG. BANG. BANG. The knocking on the front door grew louder with each thud. Aaron had been doing his best to ignore the sound for the past five minutes as he rushed around moving a few sets of fall clothes, toiletries, television, and the medical supplies the doctors ordered from their bedroom upstairs to the guest room downstairs, as the stairs would prove difficult for Jordan while he had crutches. *What else do we need?*

More banging. *God damn it!* There was absolutely no one who would knock on the door that Aaron had any desire to interact with right now. He had sent one text message to Troy, at Jordan's urging, telling him not to contact him again. Troy responded with a plea to listen to his side of the story but saying he would let Aaron come to him. Which would happen sometime in the vicinity of never and when hell froze over. *Because what the fuck could Troy possibly say to justify leaving Jordan in a foreign prison to die? Worse still, proving that he was dead? Nothing. There is nothing that could justify such cruelty.* Besides, Aaron was just biding his time until Jordan gathered enough evidence to convict Troy. Aaron didn't know how to do that, but he and Jordan would figure it out. Troy would not be stupid enough to show up here. Not with the remote possibility that Jordan would be home. Or the knowledge that Jordan and Aaron kept a gun in the house, and neither was afraid to use it.

So, who else would be at the door? The reporters dying for a quote from the rescued POW and his spouse? No, thank you. Aaron had a specific, completely fabricated script from the military detailing what to say to the media if he deviated from no comment. But the higher military officers understood by now that he did not do what he was told just because they asked. Smart bunch.

Aaron's phone buzzed with a text from his brother, Chris.

Please answer the door.

Chris, along with everyone else, had abandoned Aaron after he refused to attend Jordan's funeral. With Jordan showing up, clearly not dead, Aaron had been right all along. Not that anyone important had acknowledged this.

Aaron sighed, walked through the living room, and swung open the heavy wood to find his brother on the other side. "What?"

"I'm sorry," Chris said. "Can we talk?"

Rolling his eyes, Aaron stepped aside. "Make it quick. I don't have much time."

"What are you doing?" Chris sat on the arm of the couch.

"Setting up the downstairs room for me and Jordan. The doctor is releasing him in a few hours," Aaron answered.

"Need help?"

Yes, Aaron needed help with everything, but he was not about to admit that to someone who had turned against him when he needed the most support. "I've been doing fine. Thanks for the offer though."

"Look, man, I'm sorry," Chris told him, rubbing his face. "I saw Jordan on the news the other day, and I damn near fell out of my seat. How could you have known?"

Aaron shrugged. "I can't explain it, other than I just did. The story didn't add up, which I told you."

"You told everyone. We thought you were..."

"Crazy? In denial? Yeah, I know." Aaron swept his hand through his hair and noted the passage of time since he left the hospital.

"But you weren't... You actually knew. How?"

And he still doesn't listen. "Do you want a formula? I don't know how, except that nothing made sense. Didn't feel right."

"The media said he broke out of the prison and got on a plane with rich Americans."

"Yes. It did."

Chris tilted his head to the side. "How did he manage that? Why didn't he go to the embassy?"

"All I know is what's made public. So, I heard the same story you did." Not completely true. Jordan had told him bits and pieces about the prison nurse helping him escape. However, he did not have a complete story. Nor could he offer one to his brother if he did. Because on his best day, Chris was neither the most trustworthy nor responsible person. Aaron shook his head. "I can't blame you for not getting it. No one did. But I also don't know who I can trust, since no one supported me when the chips were down."

"Except Troy."

Aaron had to fight not to puke at Chris's words. But again, Chris didn't know. "We'll go with that."

"Did I miss something?"

"Nothing I can share."

Chris stared at him for a few moments and nodded. "Please. I screwed up. Let me make it up to you. What do you need? There has to be something."

Aaron opened his mouth to refuse again, but then remembered. "Food. I haven't gone grocery shopping. If I give you cash and a list, would you go?"

"Absolutely." Chris followed Aaron into the kitchen. "Um... Dad said—"

Aaron tensed. "I could not care less if he claims to be sorry or whatever. He crossed a line. I don't want to hear it."

Chris patted his shoulder as Aaron handed him a very detailed list and cash. "All right. I'll see you in an hour."

Sadness washed over Aaron as he watched his brother walk out of the door. He had no one to trust, except for his struggling husband and his father-in-law. And it would be unfair to complain about anything to the man who survived as a POW or the elderly man who'd had his world turned upside down twice in the last month. So, Aaron would handle it alone. What choice did he have?

"WHERE ARE YOU going?" Jordan asked, jolted awake by the creak of the bedroom door two weeks later.

Aaron paused and took a few deep breaths before turning around. "I can't sleep, so I was going to the living room to get some work done."

"Can you work in here?"

"I don't want to disturb you," Aaron answered. "You need rest."

"I can't sleep alone."

The truth was Jordan couldn't do much alone. Aaron thought sleep would be something he could handle. *Not his fault.* "Let me get my computer and headphones. Do you need anything while I'm up?"

"No, thanks. Angel?" Jordan called when he reached the doorway. Aaron glanced over his shoulder. "I'm sorry."

"Don't worry about it." His frustration melted at the sound of the nickname. Aaron gathered his computer from the other room, even knowing that work would be difficult with Jordan awake. Jordan's PTSD was worse than they anticipated, but why they'd underestimated the effects of near isolation in a foreign prison was beyond Aaron's comprehension.

Sitting cross-legged on the bed, Aaron situated his laptop in front of him. Jordan placed his head on Aaron's lap and raised his eyes in question. He required constant contact, or at least for someone, usually Aaron, to be in his sight, which was hard for Aaron to adjust to. But really, how could he complain? Aaron leaned down and kissed Jordan's forehead. "Try to get some sleep."

Jordan nodded and shut his eyes. "Love you, Angel."

"Love you too. Always." Aaron stroked his husband's face with one hand and typed slowly to minimize noise with the other. He felt like the most selfish human being in the world for getting impatient when Jordan needed him the most. Sometimes, though, he worried that things would always be like this. Aaron yearned for the ease of the past...

Jordan feathered kisses on Aaron's naked leg, pulling him from his thoughts. "For someone without a lot of padding you're always so warm."

Aaron pushed the computer to the side and stroked Jordan's cheek. "Thought you were tired?"

"I was, but you're warm, and sleep is less appealing than crawling into that warmth." Jordan's lips changed direction toward his hip. His smoldering brown eyes were alight with a passion Aaron had yearned to see.

As Jordan nipped Aaron's hip bone, Aaron's cock jumped to life. "Ugh, Jor, please don't tease."

"Promise, not a tease," Jordan replied, nudging him down and kissing up his torso. "Fuck, Angel, you taste like heaven."

"Yeah? And what exactly does heaven taste like?" Aaron questioned.

A devilish smile, unlike any Aaron had seen since prior to Jordan's deployment, crept onto Jordan's face. He stuck out his tongue, collected a few drops of Aaron's precome, and leaned up to press their lips together. As he opened his mouth, Aaron savored his own juices. "That's what heaven tastes like."

"Can we?" Aaron whispered.

"I don't see why not, considering I broke my ankle, not my cock."

Aaron's gaze drifted to Jordan's casted leg, which compromised his mobility. "Top or bottom?"

"Top," Jordan asserted, more forcefully than necessary.

"Lie on your back." Aaron assembled some pillows under Jordan's foot. He stopped to stare at his husband, lying naked before him. Maybe Jordan had some extra scars. Maybe his muscles were less defined under his dark skin. But he was here. Ready to drive into Aaron's waiting hole. Jordan's hard cock bobbed in anticipation. Aaron smiled. "You're gorgeous."

Jordan extended his arms to embrace Aaron. "Show me, please."

Aaron rooted through the nightstand and found a bottle of lube. Why it was there, he couldn't say. Then again, Aaron was not about to spend a lot of time contemplating it. He met Jordan's eyes as he kissed over his torso, treating the smooth areas the same as his rough scars. "Perfect," he said as he reached Jordan's face.

"Don't lie to me."

"I never have." Aaron kissed his pillowy lips. "Now, I'm going to make love to you. Do you know why?"

Jordan bit back his returning smile. "Because there's no romance in fucking?"

Aaron answered by caressing lube onto Jordan's cock and straddled his hips, easing down until he bottomed out. They locked eyes as Aaron's channel hugged Jordan's pulsing member. Neither moved for a long moment. Fusing their lips together again, Aaron knew this was real. For the first time since Jordan arrived home, Aaron wasn't waiting to wake up. Had he been, the thrust Jordan gave would have done it.

"Out of your head," Jordan commanded. And that did it. They thrust in sync, ending with mutual eruptions. And following a cleanup, Jordan snuggled into Aaron's arms, where he fell back to sleep.

Yes, I'll take his clinginess to get that in return any day, Aaron thought with a kiss to Jordan's hair.

Chapter Twenty-Three

"DO YOU NEED help?" Aaron asked Jordan while he was dressing in his army uniform on the day of a meeting with Bryant and other military officials three weeks later.

Jordan offered a half smile as he worked his pants over his cast. "You cannot get impatient with me when I ask for help and when I don't. Pick one."

"I don't—" Aaron began to protest but stopped at the appearance of Jordan's raised eyebrow. "Sorry."

"Don't worry about it," Jordan responded. Now that his ability to move around with crutches was improving, he relied on Aaron less for daily activities, but not for peace of mind, something Aaron had been great about providing. The dependency of the first few days home from the hospital had been difficult for them both. Aaron had only left him a few times to run errands. Then his dad had stayed with him, which was as close to useless as one could get because Jordan was not about to ask his elderly father for assistance going to the bathroom. He had to keep that much pride. But staying made Elliot feel included.

Aaron sat down next to Jordan. "I'm asking if you need help because showing up late to an army meeting could have pretty severe consequences."

"What? Are they going to fire me? I quit, several times." No, he would not reconsider his decision to resign after being held captive in the Middle East. He had to emphasize this to his commanding officer repeatedly. For some reason,

Colonel Bryant thought the experience would endear him to the military. Jordan grunted at his pant leg. "Shouldn't be this damn hard." Though he could have been describing leaving military service as easily as dressing.

"Speaking of quitting, I refused to allow them to give you a 'posthumous' promotion." Aaron inserted the air quotes, and Jordan's smile turned genuine.

He leaned over and kissed Aaron's lips. "Thank you." A promotion to major may have meant another three years in the army. Not a chance Jordan was willing to take.

"You're welcome. The honor of the title was not worth the consequence once I found you." Before Jordan could question again how he knew, Aaron gestured to his foot. "What happens if you cut the bottom?"

"They don't like the uniforms altered." The rest of the uniform was two sizes too big, but that did not help Jordan to fit the tapered bottom over his cast.

"But...as you said, you quit. It shouldn't make a difference what they like."

Jordan stared at the stubborn opening once more. "All right. Can you bring me the scissors?" Standing up to hunt for them was not worth the effort.

Kneeling in front of him, Aaron cut the fabric and rolled it to the top of his cast.

"That felt like such a rebellious act," Jordan muttered, eliciting a laugh from Aaron. "Ready?"

Aaron handed him his crutches and waited while he balanced on them. "Yeah, let me grab my computer, so I can work in the library while you talk."

Jordan checked his pockets, wallet, cell phone, and military ID. He had spoken to Bryant and the military investigator twice each. Today Jordan and Bryant were meeting to address any remaining questions he had.

"Any chance Troy will be there?" Aaron asked as they settled in his car.

Fucking Hart. Jordan coached his pulse to steady after the mention of the asshole's name. "Only Bryant and me."

Aaron reached over and squeezed his hand. "Are you mentioning him yet?"

"No. I'm still hoping they figure it out on their own."

"How long are you willing to wait for them to do that?"

"I can't go around accusing major generals of treason without proof."

"They said lots without proof. Hell, they held your goddamn *funeral* without proof," Aaron ranted.

Jordan had read all the news articles on it over the past few weeks since he arrived home. He'd also read the public's reactions to the army's mistakes, most of whom were not forgiving. The whole thing was a surreal experience. "They have enough power to get away with that," he said quietly. "Has Hart contacted you again?"

"Yeah, letting me come to him lasted all of about a week," Aaron replied just as quietly. "But I haven't answered."

"What's he saying?"

Aaron fished his phone out of his pocket and handed it to Jordan. "You can read the text messages. Nothing important. He's begging for a chance to explain, telling me I don't understand, blah, blah, and blah."

Jordan scanned the texts on Aaron's phone. One hit him in the gut. "He called you Angel?"

"Twice. Both times I told him that was unacceptable." Aaron pulled into the lot. He turned to Jordan. "I've only ever been your Angel. And that's the way it's going to stay."

Behind Aaron's gaze, Jordan saw a deep devotion and sincerity. He kissed his lips. "Do me a favor and delete that text."

"Consider it done," Aaron promised. He held Jordan's face in his hands and brought their lips together again.

"Have I told you today how lucky I am to have you?"

Aaron shook his head. "It's me who's lucky." He glanced at the clock. "Come on, let's go in so you can finish, and then we can have crazy sex at home."

Jordan laughed, and Aaron came around to help him out of the car. Crazy sex might be stretching it, but he was thrilled with the ease that they'd picked up their intimate relationship. He left Aaron in the library of the Pentagon and rode the elevator up to the fifth floor. Jordan blocked out the image of the word "Angel" on Aaron's text message screen. *One more reason to kill Hart if I get my hands on him. Like I need another reason.* Jordan released a breath as he stepped off the elevator and knocked on the open conference room door where Bryant sat alone.

"Captain! You're looking well. Are you feeling better?"

Always with the booming. Jordan shut the door and leaned his crutches against a wall. Taking a seat, Jordan replied, "Yes, sir, I am. Thank you."

"Wonderful to hear. I brought you here to discuss some aspects of your story with you."

Jordan considered asking the lieutenant colonel if he should lower his voice to talk about sensitive matters but decided it would not be in his best interest, and the floor was empty, anyway.

"What can you tell me about Adeela Nadar?" Bryant asked.

"She's the nurse who cared for me in Afghanistan," Jordan repeated.

"Yes, what I don't understand is why she helped you so much. You claimed she defied her husband several times to advocate for you."

"Because she disagreed with the way her husband ran the prison and wanted me to live."

"So, she's an American loyalist, then?" the lieutenant colonel pressed.

"Not exactly, no," Jordan said, and Bryant raised a brow. "She did not agree with any of the leaders."

"You are a leader, Captain," Bryant stated. "What made you the exception?"

Jordan exhaled. "One of my previous decisions saved her life."

Colonel Bryant leaned forward. "How did you know you could trust her friends to get you home?"

"What choice did I have?" Jordan asked. "My method of transportation home may have been questionable. But there was no other way, as far as I could see. And no time to develop one, as I would have been executed eight hours after I climbed into the cargo truck. I trusted her because she gave me no reason not to."

"Why wouldn't you have gone to the embassy?"

"Because you thought I was dead, and I did not believe I would be well received in an enemy uniform. As far as I knew, an American representative ordered my execution, or at least did nothing to prevent it," Jordan amended quickly.

"The problem is we have not found any evidence that call was made."

Of course not. That isn't the type of thing Hart would do out in the open. "Sir, I joined the army to serve and protect the citizens of the United States and the values we hold dear. One of those values is life. Mine would have ended the next morning had I not left. I can't honestly say I care what political stance was behind that decision. Maybe Anwar Nadar lied to the guards by misidentifying the caller, or maybe the caller misidentified themselves. I don't know.

But after weeks of leaders who did not follow protocol to save my life, I hope you'll forgive me for breaking protocol to survive." Jordan stared at his superior until Bryant broke the eye contact and focused on the far wall.

"I understand your position, Captain. However, what if the pilot of the plane had been carrying terroristic materials?"

Jordan caught his gaze again. "You have trusted me for eleven years. I have been a faithful soldier every day of my service. If you're going to question anyone, why not look above you to the people making the decisions that are ultimately damning us in our mission for peace and democracy in the Middle East?"

"And how would you like me to do that?" Bryant asked.

"If it were me, sir, I would start with searching for phone records from less than obvious sources." After a moment of silence, Jordan asked, "Am I in trouble for the way I got home?" Whether Jordan received disciplinary action was ultimately up to Bryant.

Colonel Bryant raised his eyes again. "Not unless we find something untoward during our investigation. We have scheduled a date with martial court to hear your case. If we find this record before then, it will be canceled."

Jordan's heart jumped into his throat, then fell to his feet. The consequences for accepting favors from an enemy ranged from dishonorable discharge to imprisonment. The thought stole his breath.

"I trust you'll stay close between now and the end of our investigation, Captain?" Bryant questioned.

Jordan nodded.

"Very well. Please let me know if that changes and you plan to travel," Bryant said. "I would not recommend it. Dismissed."

Chapter Twenty-Four

AARON GLANCED UP from his work at the sound of Jordan's crutches squeaking as he entered the library. He planned to ask him to hang out for a few minutes while he finished the current assignment, but Jordan's tense shoulders and wild eyes signaled that would not be a wise move. Aaron closed his computer as Jordan reached the desk. "Are you all right?"

"No. I'll explain at home."

Up close, Aaron noted Jordan's crutches shook and sweat moistened his brow. *Oh, God, this is bad.* Aaron slipped the laptop into his messenger bag. Someone or something must have triggered a panic attack. Jordan had only had one since he came home from the hospital a month ago.

"Who was in the meeting?" Aaron threw the strap of his bag over his shoulder, and they made their way out of the library.

"Bryant. Please don't ask me anything else until we're home," Jordan instructed and the two of them rode in silence, Aaron's hand on Jordan's leg. Upon entering the house fifteen minutes later, Jordan sat on the couch and started undressing.

"What are you...?"

"Shut down and unplug all computers, cell phones, and tablets." Jordan handed Aaron his uniform. "Angel, please." The concern in his voice cracked the words in half.

Aaron bent down and kissed his lips. "Give me a moment." He carried the uniform to the laundry basket in their room, dropped it in, and retrieved some sweats for Jordan. Aaron had no idea what was going on, but he did not need to understand to follow simple instructions. After he disconnected all the electronics, Aaron brought Jordan the sweatpants and sat down next to him while he put them on.

Jordan dressed in the loose pants but disregarded the T-shirt. "I'm about to tell you things you don't have the clearance to hear because I need you on my side." Jordan raised his hand when Aaron opened his mouth to protest. "I know you are, but you don't have all the information, and to truly help me, you have to understand everything, or as close to everything as I can remember."

Intertwining their fingers, Aaron kissed the back of his hand. "You took off your uniform because it might be bugged?"

A ghost of a smile crossed Jordan's lips. "Yes. It sounds paranoid, but—"

"You have to be safe. I get it," Aaron assured him, and Jordan's shoulders relaxed.

"Afterward, I'll ask you to tell me what happened here. Hopefully, we can construct a cohesive plan from both stories."

Aaron swallowed hard. He dreaded the thought of telling Jordan about what led to his acceptance of his death.

"Angel," Jordan said, "I don't blame you for anything you did after they announced my death. I wouldn't have been happy to learn you were in a relationship with Hart, but I couldn't fault you for it if you were."

"I wasn't," Aaron repeated.

"I know. Promise me one thing before I start."

"Anything."

"Promise you won't doubt what I tell you, no matter how crazy it seems."

"Jordan—" Aaron lifted his hands and brushed his cheek. "—I told high-ranking military officials to go fuck themselves when they wanted me to believe you were dead without sufficient proof. I'm comfortable with crazy."

Jordan blinked. "Did you use those words?"

"Eh, more or less. You heard all about the scandal I caused. Did you think I was polite about it?" Aaron chuckled at Jordan's confusion. "I've never doubted your words or your instincts. Tell me. I'm listening."

After kissing him one last time, Jordan began, "Remember when Bryant sent me home for refusing to lead an aid mission last year?" Aaron nodded, and Jordan continued, "That's because the section of Afghanistan where the homeless were gathered was not friendly to the West. We lost soldiers every time we went near there. Bryant knew this. He said it was ordered from on high, and no amount of logic changed the major general's mind."

Major general, Aaron thought, the story coming together. "Troy."

"Yes."

"Something changed his mind though. The mission was canceled."

"No one would lead it. And the major general wasn't doing a suicide mission." Jordan rolled his shoulders back. "I have no proof of this, but I suspect he was the one to make the decision to switch you and Foster."

Aaron thought back. Keller, his former boss at the CIA, had mentioned that the decision to send his coworker, Foster, was made above his pay grade. "Troy waited until the day you left to show his face at the office."

"Yes. Here's my theory. You and I knew too damn much. We understood the Afghanistan politics, had all the background information on Nadar, and had worked with the Loya Jirga before. Foster, on the other hand, was eager to follow orders."

"But our knowledge base should have been a good thing," Aaron said. "The point of the mission was to get Americans out alive, no?"

Jordan chewed his bottom lip. "That was *our* mission, but Hart was far more concerned with covering his ass. The United States government does not appreciate military officials who work with the enemy. He had spoken to Nadar several times while I was there and insisted that I knew the whereabouts of a Muslim leader, Jalalabad."

"The one that went missing six months ago?"

"Yes. What do you know about him?"

Aaron shrugged. "Only that the Afghanistan government has a hard-on for him. They think we took him during the raid nine months or so ago."

"Did we?"

"I couldn't find him in any of our databases. He isn't a registered prisoner in Guantanamo Bay like they keep swearing he is." Aaron recalled what he could of that aspect of the mission he had studied for so long. "He's harmless."

"So, he isn't wanted by our government?" Jordan questioned.

"Not technically. They were a little suspicious when the Afghanistan government got so bent out of shape over his disappearance, but he was a well-respected Alim, and they didn't want to lose him. Can't say I blame them, honestly."

"Why the hell didn't I have this information?"

Throwing up his hands, Aaron responded, "I don't know why you wouldn't. His name was in multiple documents."

"None that I saw."

Aaron massaged his temples. "They edited the reports you got, didn't they?"

Jordan shut his eyes. "The CIA reports I saw were approved by someone higher than me."

"Which makes total sense. We don't all want to have the same information. That would be stupid." Aaron huffed. "Go on. Troy spoke to Nadar during the time you were imprisoned."

Taking another breath, Jordan said, "The day I escaped, Hart had spoken to Nadar and told him that if I wasn't going to tell him where Jalalabad was, then he should execute me."

"That fucker!" It was Aaron's turn to squeeze his eyes tight. Troy must have made that call moments before meeting Aaron at the theater. Troy's speech about how supportive he had been to Aaron made his skin crawl and stomach flip.

JORDAN TOOK HIS hand in response to the anger painting Aaron's features. "It's okay."

Aaron's eyes flew open. "No! It is *not* okay. That dirty ass-wipe not only convinced me you were dead, he tried to kill you. How is that even in the punching distance of okay?"

"Because he failed," Jordan said. Aaron swallowed hard and his shoulders trembled. Jordan pulled him into his arms as the first tears fell. His husband had managed to stay composed for most of the five weeks he'd been home, internalizing his emotions instead of going off on the rages Jordan knew he was capable of. Capable was the wrong word. Aaron needed those moments of venting to keep his head straight. To say Aaron had been dealing with a lot would be a vast understatement. Even though Aaron hadn't been dating him, Jordan observed sadness come over him when they talked about Hart. Anger he understood, but the sadness always confused Jordan.

"I'm sorry." Aaron tried to pull away, but Jordan held him tighter.

"Don't be sorry, Angel. You've done nothing wrong." Jordan rubbed his back under his shirt.

Aaron opened his mouth to protest but leaned into Jordan again. "I apologized because I can't help you if I'm out of control."

"I think you've earned a breakdown or two, love. You are a tremendous help." Jordan hesitated, then asked, "Stupid question, what prompted it?"

"I don't love him if that's what you're worried about."

"It's not. You honestly think I wouldn't have been able to tell that the day I came home?"

He smiled briefly and said, "I'm upset because Troy was the only one who stood by my side and actively supported me in my search for you. Your dad didn't try to stop me, for which I'm grateful, but I was convinced that Troy was searching. So, when he handed me the picture... My mind didn't go to Photoshop like it would have with anyone else."

Jordan loosened his grip. "Can I see it?"

Aaron raised his eyebrow. "The picture?"

Jordan nodded.

"Are you sure?"

No. "Yes. It may not have been photoshopped."

"How...?"

"Please get it," Jordan requested again. Aaron released a breath and walked to the other room.

Jordan listened as Aaron opened a drawer and removed everything. He had to concentrate on Aaron's specific movements or else his mind would drift to what he was about to see. Not many people had the opportunity to evaluate their postmortem pictures.

Aaron handed him a grainy, black-and-white photograph once he sat down again. It was him, all right. Pale, wide-eyed, but him. He squinted at the welt marks on his shoulder. "Shock." He passed the picture to Aaron, who set it facedown on the opposite side table. "The guards used canes to try to wake me from anesthesia."

"Don't they have medicine for that?" Aaron asked in horror.

"If by 'they' you mean medical facilities, yes, but Adeela was working with limited power resources."

"Power resources?"

"She didn't always get what she asked for in terms of medicine, and her husband often ordered the guards to beat me against her recommendations." Jordan shook the memory from his head. He couldn't flash back now. "When did Hart show you the picture?"

"The day I hacked into the CIA database. I don't remember the date," Aaron responded.

A smirk tugged on the corner of Jordan's mouth. "You hacked into the CIA database?"

Aaron shrugged. "I tried to login in legally, but they blocked me when I was terminated."

Jordan let a chuckle escape at the implication that Aaron had no choice except to break the law. "What did you find?"

"The newspapers mentioned that you and Parks arrived with two security guards each. However, no sources discussed all four, not even the database. I had asked Troy about the other one and he freaked the fuck out," Aaron told him.

Jordan tried to conjure the image of that day. He could not remember the names of his guards. "One guard didn't quite fit. He fidgeted during negotiations, and I was about to say something when the gun fired." Jordan turned to Aaron. "Hart got scared at the mention of that guard."

"I was on to something," Aaron said. "I should have seen it."

"Stop, Angel. I could not be prouder of how you've handled yourself." Jordan brushed his cheek with the tips of his fingers. "I'm so sorry he hurt you in this process."

Aaron embraced him. "As long as I can do this, I'll deal with the rest."

Jordan gave him a squeeze. "We need to find the missing information."

"I want to take him down too, but—"

"No but. Bryant claims to be doing a search for the government official who kept me imprisoned, but he hasn't found anything."

"Which means he's searching as vigorously as he did for you," Aaron added.

"Yeah, worse than that, though, if they don't prove that my execution was imminent, I will be court-martialed in six weeks' time for accepting favors from the enemy. He tossed the word 'terrorist' out. We're talking dishonorable discharge, if I'm lucky. Prison if I'm not." Jordan let out a shaky breath. "I can't take that chance. I would rather be dead than back behind bars."

"I won't allow either of those options. Court date in six weeks? Then we have five to compile evidence." The hysteria was gone from Aaron's voice.

"And if it takes longer?"

"We leave until we can clear your name. They don't get to take you from me for even one day."

"We can't—"

"We can. It won't be pleasant for a while, maybe, but I am not tolerating bullshit from people who don't give a damn. The only thing we can't do is allow them to put you behind bars."

"I was strongly encouraged to stay in the area during the investigation. They're watching us."

"I'm sure they are. Let them. We'll use our legal accounts to act normally and open a secret server to communicate with anyone who could help us. Would Adeela?" Aaron asked.

"If she can, yes. I also have to protect her from the terrorist label." Jordan rolled his eyes at the sheer ridiculousness of it.

"You've talked to her since you've been home, right?"

"A couple of times through email," Jordan answered.

"Then we can assume Anwar doesn't check that." Aaron sighed. "At best, she could only provide a fraction of the information. Troy has the rest."

"Yeah, I have an idea, but you'd have to agree." Aaron met his eyes in question. "What if you told him you wanted to be friends? Got him to trust you the way you trusted him?" He scrunched his face in disgust, to which Jordan responded, "I hate this too, but I can't think of any other way."

Aaron shook his head. "I'm not opposed to faking a friendship to bring him down. But he doesn't want to be friends. When I heard you outside, he was seconds from...forcing himself on me. The surge of adrenaline from the possibility of an intruder was the only thing that stopped him."

Jordan tensed as the meaning of Aaron's words hit him.

"Sorry. I..." Aaron stopped at Jordan's raised hand.

"Also not your fault. I'm glad, really."

"Glad?"

Jordan nodded. "Oh, yeah. I'm thrilled to add another reason to kill him at the first opportunity."

"Can we start there?"

"No, that will look suspicious."

Aaron sat next to him in silence, then whispered, "Should I...?"

Jordan turned back to him. "What?"

He licked his lips. "Offer myself?"

"No. Wait, that isn't strong enough. Fuck no. That bastard does not get to touch you. He sure as fuck doesn't get to touch you in pursuit of information for me." Jordan grabbed Aaron's shoulders and kissed his lips hard. "You are mine, Angel. Do you understand?"

Aaron turned one corner of his mouth up. "I'm confused. You better show me."

A ravenous growl reverberated through Jordan's chest and throat. Aaron's eyes widened as Jordan carried him to the bedroom over his shoulder. *Goddamn crutch.* He would have taken him on the couch, but Aaron's height made that uncomfortable. Jordan rolled Aaron onto the bed and sent his crutch crashing to the floor. A smile now accompanied the shocked expression.

Jordan straddled Aaron's hips and took possession of his mouth as he worked the buttons on his shirt open. "There are too many of these." He nipped Aaron's ear and neck, making no progress on the shirt. He pulled away long enough to tear open the material. Buttons flew in all directions. Aaron's pants gave little as Jordan undid the button with his teeth and pulled them down.

"Oh, fuck," Aaron moaned, kicking the pants off.

Jordan bit Aaron's nipples, pecs, and abs, adorning his torso with hickeys. No man would ever touch his husband, especially against his will. The very thought of it lit a fire in Jordan incomparable to any he experienced before. He yanked his fly down and whipped out his throbbing cock, coincidentally matching Aaron's. "You like this."

"Fuck yes!" Aaron stroked lube onto Jordan's member, as if afraid he'd forget.

Ignoring the difficulty of maneuvering around his cast, Jordan hiked Aaron's legs up and thrust in. "Listen close," he growled between gasps. "You are mine. No one else gets to have you this way." Jordan hit the gland deep in his husband's channel again and again while he cried out in ecstasy.

They moved to their shared rhythm faster and faster. Right at the edge, Jordan stopped and said, "But I'm yours too." After they exploded white-hot cream, Jordan cleaned them both up and gave Aaron a kiss. "Any questions?"

He grinned. "No, I'm good now, though, I may think of some later."

Chapter Twenty-Five

JORDAN CHUCKLED AS Aaron shifted on the couch next to him, trying to get comfortable. "Aren't you being melodramatic? It's been two days. You'd think it was the first time we had rough sex."

"First in a long time," Aaron responded.

"Fine, no more."

Without responding, Aaron signed onto Skype on their secure server. Jordan had asked to call Adeela today so they could evaluate what information she had for them. He and Aaron had decided they would wait to involve Hart until they spoke with her.

"Should I not sit so close to you?"

Jordan raised an eyebrow. "Why?"

"Muslim woman?"

Jordan shook his head. "She knows we're married. I wouldn't worry unless you get uncontrollable hormones."

"You act like you make it easy to—" Skype's ring tone interrupted Aaron's words.

Jordan pressed the green "Accept" button. Adeela's face filled the screen. "Good morning, Adeela. This is Angel," he greeted her in Farsi. "He goes by Aaron to everyone who isn't me."

"Hello, Aaron," she replied in English with a warm smile. "Jordan, you look so much better."

"Thank you. Would you prefer English or Farsi? Angel and I speak both."

"English, please. Anwar does not understand it."

"Is he there?" Aaron extended his back to his full height.

"My, you're tall! You tower over Jordan when you're both sitting." Adeela took a drink of tea. "No, he is not here. He has a phone meeting with the man from the CIA. Hart, right?"

"Yes, do they speak often?" Jordan asked.

"I believe so, yes. Hart was rather angry to hear of your escape."

I'll bet he was. "Has Anwar gotten over it?" Adeela had told Jordan that Anwar blamed her for his escape. He would not have cared so much if he were not worried about Hart no longer assisting them in finding Jalalabad.

"Once Hart offered to find him another soldier to question while he continued searching himself, Anwar forgot about being angry."

"I don't think any soldiers are going to know," Aaron suggested.

"I understand that, but let him keep trying. He stays busy and I can focus on caring for prisoners," Adeela answered.

"Speaking of prisoners, how long do you have until you have to go to work?" Jordan fingered the folder with all the information he and Aaron had compiled.

Adeela glanced at her watch. "About two hours before I go to the infirmary."

More than enough time to get a start on this.

"What do you think happened to Jalalabad?" Aaron asked her.

She met his gaze. "My guess is that he is dead, which would be fine if we could have his body back to give him a proper burial. Anwar is going crazy in his pursuit of closure." Adeela sighed and shook her head. "Hart knows more than he is saying."

"That's what we're thinking too," Jordan said. He quieted to see what she would volunteer.

"Hart claims to represent your government, but any other time we have dealt with them, it's been groups of people. And never have we started at the top."

"Did you say that to Anwar?" Aaron asked.

Adeela offered him an innocent smile. "Dear Aaron, I am only a woman. I could not hope to grasp the delicacies of political negotiations."

Aaron grinned. "Aren't you a nurse? I imagine that requires some level of education, no?"

"Yes, but that makes no difference to him. My life is far easier when he underestimates me," she replied. "How did your commanding officer respond to the story, Jordan? When we last spoke, he was still investigating."

Jordan took a breath. "Not well, Adeela. He doesn't approve of the way I got home."

Her jaw dropped. "Why does it matter? You're alive!"

"He found that argument less than convincing. He kept questioning me on what the plane carried."

"Drugs. Narcotics of some sort."

"See," Aaron cut in, "not terrorist weapons. The people buying those drugs will be far too happy to attempt an attack."

Yet, Jordan knew that answer would not comfort Bryant, as drugs were still illegal and could be sold to fund terrorist organizations.

"Is he stupid?" Adeela asked.

"Me?" Aaron's face fell.

"No. The commanding officer."

Aaron laughed. "I always thought so, but no one cares about my opinion."

"Oh, do you speak too much truth?"

"Something like that." Aaron faced Jordan. "She's fun."

Jordan rubbed Aaron's back. "Does Anwar keep a written schedule for executions?"

"Yes," she answered. "The guards and prisoners must be prepared. It's my job to ensure the prisoners are healthy enough to die."

Jordan ran his fingers through his hair. "Would it be dangerous for you to send us a copy of it?"

"No. I can scan and email it, but why?" A mixture of anger, disgust, and horror colored Adeela's face as Jordan explained Bryant's decree. "So, let me get this straight. For escaping from a foreign prison, your commanding officer might...throw you in prison?" Jordan nodded. "Has anyone informed him that he is an idiot of the highest order?"

"Jordan won't let me!" Aaron whined.

"He's following protocol," Jordan started, but Adeela interrupted.

"You are not defending the man who is, against all logic, persecuting you for escaping a situation that his people put you in! I know because you are not the same level of idiot as him."

Aaron clapped. "Thank you, Adeela."

I better enjoy having a voice because when we bring her over here, I won't be heard over these two. Jordan sighed. "Both of you, please calm down."

"You gave them my name, correct?" Adeela clarified.

"Yes, but you're safe. I promise."

"I don't doubt you." Adeela rolled her eyes. "I will get you the schedule. Will you tell me if you hear of any planned attacks?"

"Yes." Jordan hesitated. "If you're still interested, I will find a way to bring you over here."

Adeela glanced up at her hijab. "I don't know how you would convince them to help an enemy's wife."

Jordan smiled at her. "After we convince them a major general in their own army is working behind their backs, saving an enemy's wife will be cake."

She laughed. "If anyone can do it, Jordan, it's you. I should hang up. Anwar will be back soon. We'll keep each other updated."

"Adeela," Aaron called, "thank you for giving me my husband back." He hugged Jordan tight.

"You're welcome. Good luck," she said as she ended the call.

Jordan kept Aaron locked in the embrace. "I love you."

"I love you too." Aaron pressed their lips together. "I'll send Troy a message."

Jordan nodded. He had hoped they wouldn't need contact with Hart in order to gather the required evidence to convict.

For the next hour, Jordan and Aaron discussed the parameters of Aaron's "friendship" with Troy. Minimal touching, no personal information exchanged, never bring Troy there, and never allow Jordan and Troy to interact. That one was more for Troy's protection than Aaron's. Even with the guidelines in place, the thought of Aaron with the man turned Jordan's stomach.

Chapter Twenty-Six

"I'M SO GLAD you changed your mind about spending time together, Aaron," Troy said that Saturday as they met for coffee.

Aaron gave him a smile and adjusted the collar of his shirt, where a discreet live surveillance device known as a paper ant was attached. Jordan had insisted he wear it whenever Aaron and Troy were together. Aaron had a chuckle on the drive over while picturing Jordan watching on the laptop. *Maybe on the way home, I'll give him something to watch...* He blinked and turned his attention back to Troy. "Me too."

"I wish you'd let me explain," Troy started, but Aaron shook his head.

"Not necessary. I'm sure your sources lied to you." He didn't need Jordan hearing the lies.

"Exactly, I'm outraged, really. The soldiers who provided the picture are under scrutiny as we speak."

"Soldiers? As in American soldiers?" Aaron couldn't stop himself from asking.

Troy's brow moistened. "Of course. What other soldiers would I be in contact with?"

"Obviously none. Why don't we get out of here? There's a sidewalk sale on the other side of Market Street."

"Sure." Troy stood up and stretched his arms over his head, exposing his stomach.

Hopefully we can find him clothes that fit. Bare midriff tops are not meant for naked mole rats.

They left the coffeehouse and meandered down the sidewalk for a moment in silence. "How are things at home?" Troy asked.

"Great," Aaron answered.

Troy raised an eyebrow. "That's it?"

"It's true. Guess I don't have much to add." If he had someone to gush to, Aaron had plenty to add about how grateful he was every single day. But that seemed less than appropriate under the circumstances. Aaron picked up a T-shirt with SpongeBob on it. Not that it would fit him, but it would fit Jordan. And Jordan hated SpongeBob. Aaron gave the cashier his money. His skin pricked as a looming presence inched closer. He edged out of the way. "Finding anything?"

"Not my style," Troy responded, following step for step.

"Yeah? What is your style?" *Use your longer legs to put distance between the two of you.*

"I shop at Bloomingdale's and Nieman Marcus." Troy's voice heightened in the way a gay man's did when they needed to ensure that whoever they were speaking to had no doubts about their sexuality. Besides, the only style category you could put those stores into was pretentious. Then again, Aaron was not up on the fashion trends. "Ever been?"

"Uh...yeah. Bloomingdale's has great bathrooms, cloth towels and everything." His shocked expression gave Aaron enough time to move away. "What do you think of this?" Aaron held up a disco ball.

Troy smirked. "What would you do with that?"

Aaron considered a moment. "Dining room. Maybe turn it on during Thanksgiving." He laughed out loud when he thought of Jordan watching this discussion at home.

"FIRST, SPONGEBOB AND now a disco ball? Where the fuck are you getting all this money?" Jordan interrogated the computer screen. It was absolutely inconsequential to Jordan that they had enough money to support themselves, as Aaron's new job paid better than his CIA one. Incredible for how flexible his hours were. A knock sounded at the door, and Jordan leaned back in his chair to see his father's car outside. "Damn it." He removed his headphones and minimized the video window. Jordan grabbed his one crutch and hobbled to the door. "Hey, Dad. Everything all right?"

"I need to speak with you," Elliot said as Jordan let him in.

"Um...right now?"

"No, son." Elliot took a seat on the couch and rested his cane beside him. "I drove over here for something that can wait."

Jordan sat across from his father. "What's wrong?"

"Where's Aaron?"

Now, I understand why answering a question with a question is so annoying, and where I picked up the habit. "He's buying nonsense downtown."

"He isn't alone." Elliot shook his head. "I can't tell you how disappointed I am in him. I cut him some slack while you were away, but... Why are you shaking your head at me? I saw him, Jordan. I can prove it."

"You don't have to. I am well aware of who he is with and what nonsense he is buying."

Elliot's forehead scrunched in confusion. "You're all right with that?"

"No. We have no use for a disco ball."

"And who he's with?"

Jordan chewed his bottom lip. "We might have a use for him. Rather, we have use for the information he is in possession of. And we can't seem to get that information without him."

Elliot stared at Jordan, swallowed twice. "Aaron is not cheating on you?"

"No, but I can't say more than I have because you should not be implicated in this."

Inhaling deeply, Elliot pulled himself to his feet. "All right, please don't get yourself in trouble." As he was almost out the door, he turned and added, "I am more than happy to give you pointers on how to eliminate him once you have what you need."

Oh, I have quite a few ideas on elimination. Though Jordan often questioned if he would follow through if given the opportunity. More than likely, he'd be satisfied to see the law handle Hart. Jordan shut the door behind his father. He would not be dragging *him* into this mess.

He hobbled back to the computer and enlarged the video, but didn't bother to re-engage the sound when he saw Aaron climbing into his car. He was perfectly capable of driving the few blocks home without Jordan monitoring him. Jordan opened Google Chrome to check Facebook. He got so lost in cat pictures and motivational memes that he nearly jumped out of his skin when Aaron entered the house swinging two bags against the wall and door.

"What are we going to do with a disco ball?" Jordan greeted him as he stood and made his way to the couch, noting the passage of ten minutes. "And don't say Thanksgiving. My father will have a seizure."

Aaron laughed, set the bags on the opposite couch, and cuddled up to Jordan. "How about the bedroom? We would have to turn it off to sleep, but it might enhance the mood during sex."

Jordan eyed him but wrapped his arms around Aaron's angular frame. "I missed the last few minutes. Anything interesting happen?"

"Damn! That was the best part. I spent the ride home teasing you."

"Teasing?"

Aaron leaned down and pressed their lips together. "Yeah, I was describing all the things I wanted to do with you."

"Yeah? Any of them involve me ravaging you for buying a disco ball?" Jordan threw back, kissing his neck.

"I'm surprised you're so caught up on the disco ball. I thought you'd be more upset about the T-shirt."

"That's cheap and there are many uses for shirts."

"Even a SpongeBob one?"

"Mm-hmm, dishrag. Seems fitting." Jordan nudged Aaron onto the couch and groaned as they struggled for places to fit their limbs. "We need bigger furniture."

"Wouldn't fit in here," Aaron answered. "Bedroom?"

Jordan should ask again what he missed, and say no anyway because Aaron wasted money, but rational thought left him as his husband went back to work on his neck. "Okay, yes, bedroom." He stumbled up.

"You all right?" Aaron grabbed his arm to steady him.

Jordan's face heated as he balanced on his crutch. "Yes. I can't wait to get this cast off."

"You're doing better with one crutch instead of two. That's an improvement."

"Sure." Small consolations kept Jordan's spirits up in the long term, but his lack of easy mobility still frustrated him. Aaron nipped behind Jordan's ear, preventing his descent to self-pity. The crutch thudded to the floor, but Aaron caught him around the waist before Jordan's balance could be compromised.

"I got you," Aaron whispered, easing Jordan onto the bed. He crawled to the other side of him so they faced one another. "You're gorgeous."

Closing his eyes, Jordan shook his head. He was well aware of his scars. Despite not doubting Aaron's attraction to him, he had no illusions of universality. "Your opinion is the only one that matters to me."

Aaron reached over and stroked Jordan's cheek. "I love you."

"I love you too." Jordan slid his tongue along the crease of Aaron's lips, unzipping them. As their tongues met, the urgency from the living room shot through them again and Jordan pinned Aaron to the bed.

"Uh..." he began.

Jordan cocked his brow at Aaron's hesitation. "What's wrong?"

"I can't...um...bottom."

"Oh." Jordan loosened his grip and released a breath. He considered asking why, but it didn't make a difference. If Aaron said he couldn't bottom, the reason could be physical or emotional, but the outcome remained the same.

"Is that a problem?" Aaron asked. "It never has been."

Not prior to leaving for this last deployment. Up until then, Aaron may have shown a preference for receiving, but Jordan enjoyed both. Yet, he hadn't bottomed since arriving home. It meant giving up more control when Jordan was just gaining it back. Which was a stupid way to think about it since they never attributed sex to power in their relationship. But if it did come down to power dynamics, wouldn't his husband be the person to risk losing control with? *Only for Angel.* "We can try."

Aaron knelt between Jordan's legs, shooting heat out of his slatted eyes. "No try. I have some tricks to ensure success."

"Oh, do you?" Jordan challenged.

Licking his lips, Aaron replied, "I do." He stripped his shirt over his head and dropped it on the floor.

"Mm, that's a start." Jordan slid his hands up and down Aaron's bare torso.

"Thank God that wasn't all I had planned." Aaron helped Jordan out of his shirt and pants. Jordan reached to unbutton Aaron's jeans, but Aaron grabbed his hand and kissed it. "I'm not there yet."

The speed change made Jordan's head spin. They weren't going to have fast, possessive sex. Aaron seemed intent on taking his time. "Angel," Jordan murmured.

"Yes, love?" Aaron embraced him.

Jordan tightened his hold and buried his face in Aaron's neck. Aaron retained his familiar scent after all these years. He yearned to surround himself in the ultimate comfort he found there. "I need you."

The heat of lust now mixed with that of love. "I've always needed you. Always will," Aaron told him, trailing kissing from Jordan's lip in a zigzag pattern to his navel.

"Ugh!" Jordan bucked his hips toward Aaron. In a plea for what, he did not know.

Aaron shimmied out of his jeans and grabbed the lube from the top of the nightstand. The two men drank in each other's naked truth. After he brought Jordan's legs to his chest, Aaron applied the lube to them both.

They connected bodies, hearts, and minds in a way that Jordan had not known they were missing. But as they released their pleasure, he knew he wouldn't give it up for anything again. Aaron cleaned them up and snuggled against Jordan. "What else did I miss? Besides teasing?" Jordan questioned, and Aaron sighed. "See, now, I think you were just trying to distract me with sex."

"Not *just*. We made love for many reasons. Distraction was a fringe benefit at best."

Jordan moved his hand away from Aaron's side.

"Hey, no, that's not fair!" Aaron protested. "Withholding affection is emotional manipulation."

"Withholding information is worse."

"Nothing bad. I set up a time to hang out with Troy two Saturdays from now."

Jordan blinked and put his arm around him again. "That's the only way to collect the evidence."

"We're watching movies at his house."

"No."

Aaron squinted at him. "Did you tell me no?"

"Uh-huh, and I'll do it again. No. You are not spending time alone with him at his house," Jordan said.

"How else am I going to find documents, files, communication records, or anything else we need?"

"It isn't safe. Besides, you know what 'watch movies' means."

"That's what you're worried about?" Aaron pulled away and stared down at him. "You don't trust me."

"I do. To the ends of the earth and back. I don't trust him as far as I can throw him, and I can't throw him into the pits of hell where he belongs, at least not from across town." Jordan sat up.

"Jor, listen to me. There is no point in spending time with him if not to get access to these accounts. That video recording won't do shit to prove his guilt. It's illegal, and won't stand up in court," Aaron pleaded. "We need something concrete."

Jordan blew out a breath. "Unless he hands you the evidence, you're obtaining it illegally."

"Right, but bank statements and email exchanges from the enemy are going to be a lot more convincing than vague references to his sources."

"Damn you for being smart and hot," Jordan muttered and kissed him. "You will wear two paper ants, and if I lose signal, I will show up."

Aaron smiled. "Yes, sir."

Jordan blinked. "I think you want round two in opposite positions."

Shrugging, Aaron replied, "I wouldn't argue..." He may have had more to say, but Jordan's cock filled his mouth.

Chapter Twenty-Seven

JORDAN RODE THE elevator up to the fifth floor of the Pentagon for a meeting with Colonel Bryant that Thursday. A meeting that he hoped would go better than their last. He hobbled out of the elevator on his crutch, counting down the days until the cast came off. Four now. Jordan entered Bryant's office, and they exchanged pleasantries.

"Captain, I called you here today to share some great news, but first, I wondered if you could confirm the placement of the prison where you were kept in Kabul." Bryant slid a map of the Afghanistan capital over to him.

Jordan scanned the paper and placed his finger on a spot in Shar-e-Naw. He had memorized a similar map while planning his escape.

"How far from the American Embassy did you say it is?"

"About a half a mile," Jordan replied, wondering if Bryant was going to ask him to repeat his escape plan again.

"Perfect!" A wide grin spread over his commanding officer's face. At Jordan's confusion, Bryant explained, "We're developing a mission to bomb the prison."

Jordan blinked. "Is that the good news?"

"Yes! I know you believe that an American government official ordered your death, but it makes far more sense that Nadar and his constituents manufactured the story so you would doubt your government," the lieutenant colonel told him.

"You're…bombing the whole prison? What about the civilians?" Jordan asked once he could moisten his mouth enough to get the words out. *What about Adeela?*

"The prisoners? We'll raid the facility first and rescue them. The only people left will be Nadar, his wife, and the people following his orders."

"His wife? What has she done?"

"Control yourself, Captain! What has gotten into you?"

"Anwar Nadar is a terrible man who deserves to be prosecuted, but are we really in the business of killing by proximity now? Is that the America we've been fighting for? If so, thank God I got out." Jordan stared him down.

"Tell me why she would not be guilty of aiding him."

Because she's not. "She saved my life multiple times, sir."

"That's her job."

Jordan shook his head. "Her job is to keep the prisoners alive. She made a choice to give me the best medical care she was able. She would not have done that if she had been actively working against the American agenda. Adeela Nadar is not the enemy."

Colonel Bryant shuffled papers into a folder. "You make wild statements that I have increasing problems believing, but because we have worked together so long, I will give you a shot to prove it. If she will help us in our mission, she will be spared."

"And given United States citizenship?" Jordan asked.

"If she so chooses, yes, but if she won't aid us, I don't want to hear any more protests from you. Are we understood?"

"Yes, sir." Jordan hobbled out after his commanding officer dismissed him.

Did I really say that about the United States? That could have gotten me disciplinary action in of itself, he thought as he rode down in the elevator. He walked through the hallway leading to the library to find Aaron with headphones on, the veins in his forehead signaling deep concentration. Jordan sat next to him, torn between pulling him from his work so they could go home where he'd be able to talk to Adeela, and letting him finish. He passed the time by playing on his phone.

"Hey, I didn't see you there," Aaron told him after a few minutes. "How did it go?"

"I seem to have borrowed your mouth." Jordan offered a small smile. "I'll explain later. Are you all right to leave?"

Aaron scanned his work. "I can do the rest at home." They packed up and made their way to the car.

Once there, Jordan recounted the conversation with Bryant.

Aaron's pause filled the car with a heavy silence that Jordan feared contained judgment, but at last, he said, "I'm proud of you. But...what are you going to tell her?"

"The options are describing the exact plan of attack, instructing her to get out of the area, or asking her to help." If Jordan went with option one, he was committing treason. On the other hand, option three asked the same of her. Option two appeared to be the best solution, but that only offered her short-term safety, unless the American government had proof of her innocence. But how could Jordan ask her to do something he was not willing to do? "What if I gave her the choice of what she's told?"

"Do you think there is even a fraction of a possibility that she would choose less information?" Aaron threw back. "And you missed an option. You don't have to say anything at all to her."

Jordan huffed out a breath. "I can't risk her dying because I did nothing."

Aaron stopped the car in front of their house and smiled at him. "I know, and I respect you for that too. If it makes you feel better, one and two would have the same end result, she'd be out of harm's way without aiding an enemy. Option two has the advantage of keeping your conscience clear."

"If she hides, they'll search for her."

"*That* makes sense to tell her." Aaron kissed to Jordan's cheek.

They walked into the house and Jordan signed onto their secure server while Aaron resumed work a few feet away. Jordan held his fingers above the keys, trying to come up with the right words for the email. He finally decided on: *Please call me on Skype. It's important.* After a glance to the clock and simple math, Jordan deduced that it was around 11:00 p.m. there. What if she couldn't get back to him until the morning because Anwar was there? What if she said no? That was a possibility Jordan had to come to terms with.

Skype's notification box popped up on the bottom of his screen. He answered the call with a shaky inhale. "You're up late."

Adeela's smile contained a hint of sadness and the crevasses on her face appeared deeper under the fluorescent light. "I must be awake when Anwar comes home. His meeting will run until the early hours," she replied. "What's important?"

Jordan opened and closed his mouth several times. "I can get you out."

"How?" The question seeped with hopeful trepidation.

He glanced at Aaron, who took off his headphones and sat next to him.

"Hello, Aaron, do you approve of this plan?" she asked. They had explained the fact that Aaron had worked with Jordan until the last deployment, which made her more comfortable sharing information.

"I approve of anything that ensures your safety. We're not sure if you will agree though." Aaron squeezed Jordan's hand.

"Go on," she prompted.

"My commanding officer does not believe that an American official sanctioned my death, or those of the five POWs who were killed prior to my mission, because they haven't found proof in the surface sweep they conducted," Jordan explained. "Therefore, they're placing the blame solely on Nadar and the people who work for him."

"Because blame can't be shared," Adeela commented.

"That, and the US is never wrong." Jordan rolled his eyes for effect, but his pulse raced. *What the fuck am I doing? I should have written out a script.* "The army is planning an attack on the prison. If you help, you'll be given full United States citizenship."

"When? Help who?"

"I don't know when. The officer may have told me had I not lost my mind at him. And...help the United States Army." Jordan's heart jumped to his throat.

"If I don't help enemy forces to attack my country, I will die?" Adeela asked, her tone measured.

Jordan met her eyes across the computer screen. He had no answer for her.

She took several deep breaths. "What would you do?"

Jordan answered the easiest question anyone he had been asked him all day. "I would live, and I would want those I cared about to live, by any means necessary."

"Can you guarantee me I will?"

"If you provide information that helps us capture Anwar and the guards who tortured and killed the Americans, then yes, I will personally make sure you live." Jordan had no idea how, but he would find a way to ensure her safety. Fear and uncertainty flashed across her face. He had no words of comfort to offer.

Though it appeared she didn't need comfort. Her expression changed to one of peace and acceptance. "All right, Jordan, I trust you. Tell me what to do." Adeela's words lifted a weight off him.

Chapter Twenty-Eight

"TAKE YOUR PAIN pill," Aaron told Jordan, who limped around on his walking boot nine days after having the cast removed.

"Can't if I'm going to drive," Jordan replied, taking a seat on the couch with his laptop.

Aaron arranged his DVDs in their holder, placing the shortest up front. Those would be the ones he offered to watch with Troy. "You aren't driving. I'm going to complete this mission while you edit your pro-con list of the PhD schools for the hundredth time." What Jordan would really be doing was watching the surveillance video.

"I have to be able to drive if the need arises."

Aaron bent down and kissed him. Jordan had been in more pain since they removed the cast than he had in the weeks prior. "It won't. I'll be fine. I have Fluffy here if anything happens." Aaron patted his sidearm, tucked into his pants' cargo pockets. He was grateful to have obtained his concealed weapon license before the laws became ridiculous.

Jordan laughed and kissed him again. "It disturbs me that you named your pistol Fluffy."

"Yeah, but it also makes you laugh. Fair trade." Aaron touched the paper ant on the middle of his back and the one on the top of his jeans while watching Jordan's computer screen light up with images of what was behind and in front of him.

"I only want you to do this once. So, last time, what's the plan?" Jordan asked.

"I go early because I know he's having computer problems." Aaron paused when Jordan raised his hand.

"How do you know he's having computer problems?"

"I've been monitoring the email with a virus I sent from my 'hacked' account. He opened and downloaded it." Aaron smiled. "Because I'm a good friend, I'll offer to fix it. Unfortunately, by the time I arrive, his hard drive will be destroyed. At some point, he'll leave the room. I'll take that opportunity to copy the backed-up files onto my USB stick and then destroy his external drive."

"What about his email accounts?"

"His passwords are taped to the bottom of the desk drawer. I'll take a picture of the paper with my phone."

Jordan pulled him down for another kiss. "I love you. Be safe."

"I love you too. And I will," Aaron said, grabbing the keys and leaving the house. Upon arriving at Troy's, Aaron did one last check of his pockets: phone, keys, flash drive, and Fluffy. He picked up the DVD holder from the passenger-side seat and strode to the door.

"Aaron, you're early!" Troy greeted him.

"I'm sorry. Didn't you say one?" Aaron asked with fabricated confusion.

"Um, maybe, I thought it was two thirty."

"Oh. Two thirty? That would be a shame. I need to get home by five to make the mashed potatoes for dinner tonight. My father-in-law is coming over." Aaron stopped himself from providing too many details as that was a well-known sign of a liar. He would avoid tipping Troy off if he could prevent it. "I can come back if it's a bad time."

"No. No. Come on in," Troy rushed out. "Just give me a few minutes to finish updating my computer. It's been giving me problems."

"What's wrong with it?"

"It's not opening or saving documents like it's supposed to. So, I'm trying a system reboot." Troy glanced from Aaron to the computer. "I think your email was hacked."

"Oh, shit, you're right. Someone else mentioned that. Can I help?"

"Would you mind? I'm not great with that stuff."

"Not a problem at all. It's sort of my fault," Aaron told him.

"No, it's not."

"Still, I don't mind."

"Are you sure? I don't want you to have to work on your day off."

"What are friends for?" Aaron smiled sweetly at him. A sense of this being too easy washed over him, but he pushed it away as he logged into the computer on safe mode. Troy had already run the usual scans. Found nothing. Aaron ran them again to appear busy. "The antivirus software needs to scan your external drive."

"The virus couldn't reach the external drive," he replied too quickly.

That's where I need to be. "Yes, it can, especially if the drive was connected to the computer." At his hesitation, Aaron added, "Trust me, Troy. Your porn collection will shock me far less than it would the Geek Squad."

Troy laughed. "You're right. Taking it to the Geek Squad is definitely not an option." He connected the drive. "I need a drink. Can I get you anything? Beer, wine, smoothie?"

"Smoothie?" Aaron cocked his eyebrow.

"Yeah, I make a wicked banana-strawberry blend."

"I'll try some of yours. Thanks." Not that Aaron would drink anything the man gave him, but it would keep him busy for a while. After taking the promised picture with his phone, Aaron inserted his USB drive into an appropriate slot and scanned all the documents on the external drive. He copied them onto the flash drive and tucked it safely away in his pocket. He leaned back in the chair to check that Troy was still occupied, then transferred the virus from Troy's computer onto the drive where the files were. A few more keystrokes and... Blue screen of death. Bingo. "Oh, shit, Troy. I'm sorry."

"What did you do?" Troy closed the distance between the kitchen and living room.

"I ran the virus program that you had started," Aaron told him. He became aware of the weight of the gun in his pocket as Troy stared fire at him.

"How did a virus protection program set off a virus?"

"Worsened it, actually. It had already been harming the system, but between the updates and trying to remove it... I'm sorry." *Please don't panic, Jordan. I got this.*

Troy took a few deep breaths. "I guess it would have happened to anyone. I'm sorry too, but I have to get someone else to come over and take it apart. I store a lot of very important files on there."

"Doesn't the CIA have a tech department? They'd want to keep your important files safe." Aaron pushed the USB drive further into his pocket.

Troy bit his lip. "It's, um, not my work computer. I'd rather them not see that I keep important files on more than one machine. You know how they get about security. We wouldn't want secret op information falling into the wrong hands."

"No. We certainly wouldn't." Aaron gathered his keys and DVDs, and added, "We'll hang out another time."

"Absolutely." Troy glanced from Aaron to the computer.

"Sorry again. I didn't mean to." Aaron left after Troy offered his reassurance once more.

Chapter Twenty-Nine

JORDAN WRAPPED AARON in a hug as soon as he entered the house. "You are crazy, and I love you."

Aaron chuckled. "I know. I love you too." He tossed the USB drive with the files on the desk. "Now that we aren't going anywhere, you can take your Percocet while we sort through these files."

Jordan opened his mouth to come up with another excuse for why he couldn't do that, but his ringing phone interrupted him. His father. "Hold on a second," he said to Aaron. "Hey, Dad. What's up?" He didn't have time for a discussion about *Wheel of Fortune* or a lecture on seeing each other more.

"C-come 'ere." Elliot's words were faint and slurred.

"Are you at home?" Jordan grabbed his coat from the hooks by the door and motioned Aaron out.

"Y-yes. Pl-ease c-come," Elliot rasped.

"We're on our way." Jordan locked the door and hobbled to Aaron's car.

"What's going on?" Aaron turned the ignition.

"I don't know, but it's bad." Jordan contemplated calling an ambulance on the way but had no idea what to tell them.

Aaron squeezed his hand as they rounded the corner to Jordan's father's home. "We'll get through it," he promised as he parked.

Jordan jumped from the car and sped toward the house, cursing his boot the whole way. He would take ibuprofen once he sorted this situation out, to reduce the swelling if nothing else. He used his key to unlock the door while thanking God that he had accepted it when his father moved closer. "Dad!" Jordan's gaze shot around the living room but did not find his father. He advanced through the downstairs while Aaron went upstairs.

Elliot followed the same schedule every week. At 3:00 p.m. on a Saturday, he should be sitting in his recliner watching the History Channel. Jordan opened the bathroom door. Nothing. Kitchen was clear. He almost left, but spotted a note on the kitchen table, reading, *STOP. NEXT TIME HE'S DEAD.*

His blood ran cold. "Angel!"

Aaron came to the top of the stairs, placed his finger to his lips, and pointed to the phone in his hand. "Yes, on 13 Mango Street. My father-in-law fell and appears to be having a stroke." He started ticking off stroke symptoms: one-sided numbness, confusion, and blurred vision.

Jordan approached the steps, but Aaron shook his head.

"Someone has to let the EMTs in. I was talking to my husband." He paused and added, "We'll be here. Jordan will open the door." Aaron hung up. "Your dad was in the master bathroom peeing when he fell. He's conscious, embarrassed, and a little confused. The EMTs will arrive momentarily. I'm going to clean him up before they get here. Please stay there. I don't want you to get hurt walking up the stairs." Aaron turned away.

Jordan called, "Angel." Aaron faced him again. "This was not a natural occurrence. Someone broke in." He held up the note. "In case you can't read it from up there it says,

'Stop. Next time he's dead.'" He and Aaron locked gazes for a long moment.

"Hide it."

"What? These people aren't fucking around," Jordan protested.

"Neither are we, and neither is he. Elliot knows what we're doing. He wanted to help."

"Jesus Christ, Angel, not at the cost of his life!" Jordan waved the paper in the air.

"Jor, we're so close. We can add it to the evidence." Sirens rang out in the distance. "He'll be safe in the hospital. You know he would agree." Aaron sent him a last pleading look and jogged back to the bedroom.

Hide it? Hide the evidence that someone broke into my father's house and attacked him? That was the most... logical course of action. Jordan sighed. The police would ask "Stop what?" and then Jordan and Aaron would be in trouble for collecting information illegally. *But, God, what if the person who hurt him comes to the hospital? Or where ever he went after the hospital? There would be an after... Right? What if he says something to the doctors? It's not like I can stop him or ask him to lie... Shit. Shit. Shit!* Jordan crumpled the paper up and stuffed it in his pocket, then opened the door for the EMT workers.

A few minutes later, they carried Elliot's frail body down on the stretcher. Aaron trailed behind. "You go with them. I'll meet you at the hospital," Aaron whispered as he gave Jordan a hug.

"I'm scared."

"He'll be all right. We'll make sure of it." Aaron rubbed his back while the EMTs loaded Elliot into the ambulance. "And it is not your fault."

"But..." Jordan started.

Aaron cut him off with a finger to his lips. "Troy, and whoever he's working with, obviously have a lot at stake."

Jordan nodded, kissed Aaron, and followed his dad into the ambulance. He reached over and held the elderly man's pale, wrinkled hand. "I'm here, Dad," he said while the medical technicians set Elliot's IV and oxygen mask in place. His blue eyes defied Jordan's inclination to coddle. *Yeah. Like Dad would allow anyone to coddle him.* After his car accident, the doctors and nurses nominated him the most difficult patient to ever stay in the hospital. Jordan was fairly certain they threw a party the day of his release.

Once the doctors had conducted preliminary tests and stabilized Elliot, he explained, through Jordan's translation, that the left side of his body went numb while he was using the bathroom. He called Jordan, who called them. End of story.

As soon as the nurses left, Elliot turned his head toward Jordan and Aaron. "Masked man... Broke in... Hit me ..." He pointed to his temple and continued, "Said...you stop." He drew in a breath. "Don't."

Chapter Thirty

TWENTY HOURS LATER, the hospital insisted Jordan and Aaron go home. They put restrictions on Elliot's visitors. Jordan had gotten maybe three or four restless hours of sleep at the hospital while the doctors tested his father's neurological activity. Had they asked, Jordan could have told them that Elliot's speech may be confusing, and the left half of his body paralyzed, but his mind was sharp. Whenever Jordan and Aaron were alone with him, Jordan's father had berated them for wasting time at the hospital with him.

"You have more important things to do than help me eat and use the bathroom. That's what the nurses are paid for," Elliot had argued.

"Let them take care of the medical stuff," Jordan had replied.

"Bullshit. You feel guilty." Elliot had huffed. "Go home."

The doctors reminded Jordan how lucky they were that Elliot was still able to communicate as well as he could. But no one had any idea what the future held for his father, beyond months of treatment and rehab. And Jordan could not accept the fact that he was not at least partially to blame. He reached into his pocket and grasped the crumpled paper. It sent a bolt of energy through him that propelled him to the kitchen to start coffee. "You can sleep," he told Aaron.

"Right. I'll heat up leftover lasagna. Please, please, take your ibuprofen."

Jordan kissed him and agreed. Ibuprofen would not hurt his ability to think or move quickly, which was no doubt why Aaron suggested it. "Where did you get a computer virus?"

"From one of my coding friends," Aaron replied. "He told me, 'only use this on someone you truly hate, because if they trace it back to you, your relationship is fucked.'"

"Fair enough." Jordan poured two mugs of coffee and brought them over to the desk. He waited for Aaron to do the same with the lasagna. "Should we each take half the files?"

"Let's see how he has the files organized." Aaron plugged the USB stick into his computer, copied the files onto the secure server, and scanned them for viruses. "What he doesn't know is that the virus destroyed all of the devices connected to the wireless router because then he can't change passwords."

"Unless he found another one in the last day."

Aaron bit his lip and logged into one of Troy's alternate accounts. "Nope. We're good." He logged out and started an incognito window before logging back in. "Paranoid, sue me." Aaron swept his hair back as they exchanged smiles. "You take the address that he corresponded with Nadar. I'll try to piece together the Jalalabad story."

The contents of Hart's hard drive pointed to the root of the problems with the Middle East for more than a decade. "Holy shit," Jordan muttered. The higher-ups promoted the man time and time again because of his congenial relations with the leaders of the Afghan government. Hart had told Nadar to kill the POWs Jordan had been sent to save. "He's been lying to everyone."

"Not technically. He is on good terms with the foreign leaders."

"Well, sure, that'll happen when you're supplying them with sacrificial soldiers." Jordan shook his head as he read about the millions of dollars Hart had accepted from the enemy for information on United States tactics. Not only the Afghan government, but the Taliban, as well. "He's playing three ways," Jordan told Aaron, who read the screen.

"Plus—" Aaron showed him his analysis. "—he's got Jalalabad here." Worse than that, Hart had been trying to convince the rest of the government that Jalalabad's disappearance indicated a terrorist plot in the making. If Jalalabad had not been on the Most Wanted list before, he was now. But...why?

The words on the screenshot the flame of anger straight from Jordan's core. Hart had taken the Muslim leader as a POW in the name of the United States and refused to notify anyone. Not the Afghan government, nor the United States government. "That bastard!" Jordan growled as memories of his imprisonment flooded his mind. Weeks of agony and isolation because Nadar disregarded the same rules as Hart. "Why is this acceptable in America?" Jordan forced himself to his feet for the first time in hours.

"It's not. Troy didn't tell anyone."

"But somewhere along the line, Hart was trained to believe that this is all right. Someone had to have told him that he could get away with this shit." Jordan paced, Aaron's gaze piercing his back.

"I don't think anyone from our government told him to convene with terrorists," Aaron said. "Did you get to the part on here about Foster?"

Foster...right. Jordan almost forgot about Aaron's people-pleasing replacement. Jordan blinked and faced his husband. "No. What about him?"

"Troy hand-selected him for the sake of being a greedy idiot." Aaron tapped the screen to enlarge the words. "Where was Foster the day you were captured?"

"He called in sick the day of the meeting with Nadar."

"According to this, Troy instructed him to make sure the capture went off."

"No. He wasn't there. That's one thing I remember well. Parks and I were relieved not to be babysitting during an important meeting."

Aaron licked his lips and kept eye contact. "Tell me what the fidgeting security guard looked like."

"I...didn't pay attention," Jordan confessed, thinking back in an attempt to bring forth a picture of the man in his mind. "I can tell you that he didn't catch my attention until we came back to the room after seeing the POWs."

"According to this exchange, Foster reported back to Troy that he took the place of another American soldier while you and Parks talked to the POWs. He ensured that Parks was killed, the POWs freed, and you were captured." Aaron paused, took a breath, and added, "Just as he ordered."

"And how much money did he receive for this?"

"Twenty thousand."

"He really should have upped the price for treason." Jordan sank down again.

Aaron put his arm around him. "It appears to be part of a long-term agreement. That continued until breaking into your dad's house yesterday."

That fucker! The block letters on the note appeared before Jordan's eyes as the reality became clearer. *STOP. NEXT TIME HE'S DEAD. He could be dead now for all these assholes know or care. They're all going down,* he swore silently and leaned into Aaron to stabilize his spinning head. "Where is Jalalabad?"

Releasing a breath, he replied, "It doesn't give a specific location."

Jordan counted backward from ten in an attempt to prevent himself from smashing the coffee table with his fist. He'd reached the number seven when an email from Adeela popped up on his phone.

Skype, please.

Right now?

Please, Jordan. It is an emergency.

The curt exchanges made the last sentence unnecessary. Her emails were normally pages long.

"Should you ask if she's alone?" Aaron questioned.

"No. She wouldn't be telling me to video call with her if she weren't," Jordan answered. "I trust her, Angel."

Aaron nodded and motioned to the computer again.

Adeela rang in through Skype before Jordan even realized it had signed on completely. "Jordan, Aaron, have you heard any more news about the attack on Anwar?"

"No, we've been busy the last few days. Why? What did you hear?" Aaron asked.

"Anwar is determined to find Jalalabad, and because his US government source insists that your soldiers know where he is, Anwar is escalating." Adeela's voice was hoarse, fearful.

"Escalating? Are they attacking the embassy in Afghanistan?" Jordan's heart tripped and sped up as she shook her head.

"Pentagon," she whispered. "Anwar and Hart are no longer friendly when they speak. Anwar thinks Hart is playing with him."

"Hart is playing with everyone. When is the attack taking place?"

"Only a few weeks from now. The Taliban is trying to take over the country again. I cannot survive that happening. Please, Jordan, you said you would get me out if I assisted the United States in their mission." Adeela's eyes were wild. "That mission will not materialize if he gets over there first."

"No, it won't," Jordan said. *Further she'll be killed no matter what.* "Are you sure you want to help?"

"Yes, yes," she answered.

I said I trust her. Now, I have to prove it. "Okay, I'm going to give you the number of Colonel Bryant. Do you know how to make calls from Skype?" She nodded, and Jordan continued, "Okay, call him in two hours. I have a lot to tell him first. Things got bad here too." He answered her raised eyebrow with, "I'll explain later. I promise."

"Thank you." She waved as she ended the call.

"Angel?"

"Yeah?"

Jordan turned toward him. "After this shit is over, how about a vacation?"

Aaron smiled. "Can it involve jumping out of a plane?"

The question ripped a much-needed laugh from Jordan.

Chapter Thirty-One

JORDAN STOOD AT attention by Colonel Bryant's office when he arrived for work that morning. "Captain, did we have a meeting?" Bryant asked, unlocking the door to admit them both.

"No, sir, but I have something to show you that cannot wait for our schedules to sync up." He extracted the binder containing the details of Hart's crimes.

"What is this?"

"The proof you've been asking for." Jordan took a seat at Bryant's scrutinizing expression. "In that binder, Aaron and I have organized the irrefutable proof that General Hart is a triple agent, working with the US and Afghan governments, in addition to the Taliban."

"Captain! That's—"

"Insane? Terrible? Disrespectful? Open the binder." Jordan let his commanding officer break eye contact first to scan the table of contents and flip through the pages. Yes, Aaron had included a table of contents. Jordan took plenty of time to mock him for that while they showered together.

Bryant's eyes widened and his face paled. "How did you obtain this information?"

"No way you would approve of, sir. I can detail exactly how it happened, but in the end, it does not matter."

"Humor me."

Jordan had really hoped that would work, though, he did not count on it. "Aaron took his files and passwords from his personal computer when General Hart asked him to fix it. We've been going through it since we came home from setting my father up in the hospital."

"A felony, Captain Collins," the lieutenant colonel said without glancing up from the binder.

"The NSA disagrees," Jordan countered. He could not allow his confidence to slip.

"That's different... Fuck!" Bryant slammed his fist on the desk. "Is this forged?" He pointed to an email exchange between Hart and Nadar.

"Nothing in there is forged. The front page has all the usernames and passwords where we accessed it," Jordan told him. "You can confirm for yourself, but if I may suggest locating Jalalabad first."

Colonel Bryant's jaw dropped as he went to the tab labeled with the Alim's name. He picked up the phone and ordered the police to arrest Hart. "Nice work, Captain."

Jordan released the breath he had been holding. "Justifiable felony?"

"Yeah. I can think of a few more to commit while we're at it. There are hundreds of pages here. What do I need to know right at this moment?"

Jordan repeated who Hart worked with, his role in the death of the POWs, Jalalabad's unlawful imprisonment, and shared the details of Nadar's upcoming attack.

Bryant opened his mouth to reply, but a knock on the door cut him off. "What?"

Two uniformed military police officers entered. "Sir, General Hart was not at home," one told him.

Flashing back to Saturday afternoon, Jordan thought about how easy it was for Aaron to access Hart's hard drive. Was he trusting or setting a trap? Jordan had no doubt that the information they compiled was accurate. So...trusting.

What would Hart do when he realized Aaron broke that trust? *Fuck!* Jordan jumped to his feet and winced at the pain in his ankle. Ibuprofen could only do so much, but he was grateful not to have taken the stronger medicine. "I need to go."

"Captain, we are not even close to done," Bryant protested.

"I know, but Hart is hurting Aaron," Jordan told him. *Not might. Is.*

"You have no basis for that. He could be anywhere..."

Jordan tensed.

"Sir, would you please take my word for it? My intuition has not been wrong once since the president appointed General Hart. I will be damned if I allow him to harm my family any more than he has." With that, Jordan strode out of the office and down the hall to the elevator.

Chapter Thirty-Two

THE WIND SMACKED the tree branches against the house. *I hope Jordan makes it back before the storm hits*, Aaron thought, blaring a heavy metal mix into his ears. Aaron logged onto his work inbox and began the first urgent troubleshooting task. It always amazed him how royally someone could screw up a website with a few errant keystrokes. He adjusted code with an additional semicolon and ampersand while bobbing his head to the beat. A chill slithered over his body.

Then a blazing heat accompanied by a bitter stench rose behind him.

Aaron whipped his headphones off with a force that disconnected them from the jack. Heavy bass and thumping drums filled the room.

Troy wrapped one arm across Aaron's chest. And held a knife to his throat with the other hand. "Don't move," he ordered, his breath as bitter as the rest of his body.

Aaron took shallow breaths in hopes of keeping his skin from making contact with the cold steel. *No swallowing.*

"Where are my files?" Troy asked.

Aaron bit his lip.

Troy slid the knife along Aaron's Adam's apple without breaking skin. "I suggest you answer me." He inched the blade away.

"I don't know what you're talking about."

The knife came back. "Think real hard, Aaron. That virus didn't accidentally appear on my external drive. As a matter of fact, the friend who searched for my files claimed it was homemade. Hard as he searched, the files weren't there."

"That's what happens with viruses. They wipe out your files."

"No, my friend analyzed the virus. The files were removed first. The virus was merely a diversion, to keep me from realizing that you stole my files." Troy lowered himself in front of Aaron. "Give them back."

"I don't have your files," Aaron whispered.

"That's a shame. If you gave them to me willingly, you would have died quickly, but now..." Troy tightened his hold on Aaron. "Now, I think you'll die the way Jordan was supposed to. Did he ever tell you about his planned execution? Maybe he didn't know." Troy brushed his lips against the side of Aaron's neck.

Puking will make him slice my throat. Don't do it.

"Nadar was going to cut major arteries. Let him bleed long enough to feel the pain before sprinkling salt in the wounds. But just as he was about to lose consciousness, Nadar would have lit his hair on fire. Each agonized scream fueling the flame." Troy kissed another spot on Aaron's neck. "I think I will start cutting you here. Sure you don't have those files?"

Inhale. Shaking will make it worse. "I don't." *Jordan does.* But Aaron wouldn't say that.

"I don't understand you. You're choosing a torturous death when this could be so easy. But, then, I guess I haven't understood much about you. Like why you kept pining for your husband when you had a better option here. I could have been good for you. Taken care of you. Even after he got back." Troy pressed the blade across Aaron's neck.

Drums and a strong metallic smell filled Aaron's consciousness.

JORDAN SCREECHED TO a halt behind Hart's black Benz. The feeling of dread he'd had at the Pentagon weighed heavier on his chest, but soon dissolved with the surge of adrenaline. Jordan ripped his walking boot off and tossed into the back seat, forcing his foot into a sneaker he kept in there for physical therapy. He patted his sidearm as he eased out of his car. Heavy metal bass shook the curtained front window. Peeking into the crack between the curtain, Jordan witnessed Troy standing above Aaron, but too far away for accurate details. Details were not important. The adrenaline provided tunnel vision as he took careful, silent steps to the back door. Jordan pulled his phone from his pocket and dialed Bryant, who answered on the first ring. Skipping pleasantries, Jordan said, "General Hart is inside my house. I need an ambulance. Actually, make that two."

"Captain, wait for the police to arrive," Bryant answered after ordering cops to their address.

"No." Jordan hung up his phone. *No* was not a strong enough response to that order. Bryant called his cell repeatedly for the seconds it took him to reach the open back door. The music vibrated the atmosphere of the house. Jordan's gaze caught two things simultaneously: the silver of a knife blade to Aaron's throat and the drop of crimson just below it.

Jordan clicked the safety off. Aimed.

Hart made eye contact with Jordan. Smiled. Dug the knife in.

Jordan pulled the trigger. And a bullet cut through the thick air.

Hart dropped the knife. Fell to his knees. Collapsed on the floor.

Jordan took three steps. Shot again.

Hart became limp, as deep crimson saturated the gray carpet.

Setting his gun down, Jordan turned his attention to his husband. The cut on Aaron's neck stretched only a few inches, but you couldn't tell from his blood-drenched shirt...or closed eyes. *No! No! Don't let me have been too late,* Jordan begged silently as he grabbed a shirt from the laundry basket next to Aaron's computer, pressed it to the cut, and shut the music off. He had never been so grateful for Aaron's aversion to folding as he was at that moment. Sirens blared in the distance.

"Angel! Angel!" Jordan called. "Please wake up. Please." Jordan dragged his bloody fingers to Aaron's pulse, where he felt a steady beat. *Thank God.*

"Jordan?" Aaron whispered. "Did you shoot me?"

Jordan chuckled and continued to apply pressure. "No, I shot the asshole trying to kill you."

"Better choice." Aaron shut his eyes again. "The smell and that noise are not helping my head."

"Noise is taking you to get stitched. Can you hold this?" Jordan asked, indicating the shirt when the ambulance pulled up in front of their house. Aaron placed his hand over it as Jordan lifted him by his neck and knees. "Don't look down." He stepped over Hart's corpse to let in the approaching EMTs, who situated Aaron on the stretcher. Jordan kissed his forehead. "Don't give them any problems, now."

"You aren't coming?"

"I have to talk to the police, but I'll be there soon," Jordan promised, with a nod to Bryant and the police officers on the scene.

Aaron's eyes widened. "Jordan isn't in trouble, is he?" he questioned Bryant. "He didn't do anything wrong."

"The police have to do an investigation. Go take care of yourself and—"

"No! I'm not leaving if you're arresting him. Troy was going to kill me if Jordan hadn't come home."

Jordan approached the stretcher. "Angel, you have to calm down. I need to explain what happened. So will you. The number one priority is you getting medical attention."

"Not without you." Aaron then addressed the police, "My husband was a POW. He can't be imprisoned or handcuffed."

After squeezing his eyes shut, Jordan released a breath. Though it probably should have, the possibility of arrest hadn't occurred to him. Jordan worked to block out a panic attack at the thoughts of being behind bars.

"No one said anything about arrest, but we have to find out why there is a dead man in your living room," the officer closest to Jordan said.

"I'll tell you why! Troy broke into our house, stood behind me with a knife, and slashed my throat. He would have killed me if Jordan hadn't stepped in." Aaron yanked the T-shirt away from his neck. Blood gushed from the wound. "Do you see? You think Troy wouldn't have taken it further? I promise you he would."

The EMTs flew to Aaron and taped gauze to the cut. "You will be restrained," one threatened.

"I want my husband with me. All you need to do is talk to him. You can do that at the hospital," Aaron demanded. "Or I won't go."

Bryant nodded at the officers. "You ride with him, Captain. We'll meet you there."

Chapter Thirty-Three

SEVERAL HOURS LATER, Jordan held Aaron's hand in the hospital trauma ward while they waited for Bryant and the police to reappear. "Don't ever try that again."

"What?" Aaron giggled for no reason that Jordan understood.

"Jeopardizing your health to accommodate my posttraumatic stress triggers," Jordan answered.

"Oh! I see. I can't hurt myself to save you from being hurt." Aaron tried to cock an eyebrow but ended up crossing his eyes instead. More giggling.

"You're high."

"Yeah, it's great. You should try it. You might be less cranky at me for doing exactly what you did." Aaron leaned on Jordan, who hugged him. "Because you don't get to feel guilty."

Jordan did though. He felt guilty for any part in hurting his father and Aaron. One thing he felt no amount of remorse for, however, was killing the rat bastard Hart. He'd done it in Aaron's defense and would have done the same to anyone holding a knife to his husband's throat. But he would be lying if he didn't admit to being relieved. The police questioned him and unanimously agreed he'd acted in self-defense. He had two other laws covering his actions, but after hearing he was not going to jail, he stopped caring what they were.

"I want to go home."

"Really?" Jordan asked. "Cuz I don't. I'm not stepping foot inside that house until a cleaning crew takes care of the mess."

"Okay, I want to get out of the hospital."

"Where'd your happy go?" Jordan threw back.

Colonel Bryant knocked and entered when Jordan yelled for him. "I'm sorry I keep leaving, but we received a call from Adeela Nadar."

Jordan shut his eyes. That's what he forgot. "I can explain..."

Bryant raised his hand. "No need, Captain. I decided that I'm not going to question your intentions or methods any longer. I don't know how you keep getting things right, but you do. You believe she's trustworthy?"

"Yes."

"Fine, then so do I. We're still looking for Jalalabad and planning the attack on Nadar's prison."

Jordan wanted to suggest that he only do one thing at a time, so something might be accomplished, but didn't think that would go well.

"Check CIA Headquarters in Langley," Aaron said.

"Why do you think he's there?"

"You'll question me, but not him? That isn't fair." Aaron puffed out his lower lip.

I would offer the excuse that he's high, but I'm pretty sure Bryant would know he'd say that regardless.

"If I had the binder in front of me, I would trace where my gut feeling originated, but I have a cut throat because you guys didn't want to cause problems with the higher-ups by asking too many questions." Aaron scratched his chin in an effort to appear contemplative and added, "Then again, there would be no need for the binder had you completed a proper investigation sooner."

"Angel..." Jordan started.

"I'm done."

Jordan wasn't sure he believed Aaron. However, the lieutenant colonel's next words convinced him he must have been dreaming.

"You're right," Bryant said. "We all would be a lot better off if we had listened when you two questioned us. The army will make sure you're compensated for the trouble."

They both thanked him. Jordan's shoulders ached, and his stomach churned. *Damn, the adrenaline crash is starting.*

"And you both earned a vacation," the lieutenant colonel continued. "We'll have a cleaning crew take care of your house as well."

"Is a vacation a great idea with everything going on now?" Jordan asked.

"Well, it would be easier for everyone if you were out of town..."

"We're not going to say anything to the media if that's what you're worried about," Aaron cut in. "But we can relax just as easily in DC as we can in North Dakota."

Jordan turned toward his husband. "North Dakota?"

Aaron shrugged. "Yeah, I don't know where that came from."

"I agree with him, sir. The advantage of staying close is that we can assist if any other problems arise," Jordan told Bryant. "Besides, I promised Adeela that I would ensure her safety, so I would like to be involved in the planning of the mission." He should have stated it as a question because he had no right to demand anything.

"I will do my best to at least show you the final plans," Colonel Bryant replied. "Rest well. You have both done your country proud." With a nod to Jordan and Aaron, Bryant left the room.

After the doctor discharged Aaron, he said, "Let's go talk to your dad."

Jordan nodded and guided Aaron into the required wheelchair.

"There is nothing wrong with my legs," Aaron muttered.

"No, but you are plenty high. Don't want you to fall." Every step Jordan took to push the chair made his body throb. His ankle had to be swollen, and the ibuprofen was decreasing the pain. But he was not sure what he expected. Jordan had put his body through a lot in last few days.

"Hey, Dad," Jordan said as he and Aaron entered his room. "How you feeling?"

"Me? He's in a wheelchair. With a bandage on his neck. What did you do to him?" Elliot asked.

Aaron wheeled over and grinned. "He saved my life from the man who has been hurting us for years." He went on to tell as much of the story as the media would.

Elliot listened and at the end of the story said, "Totally worth the fall. Can I go home now?"

"Can you take care of yourself?" Jordan countered.

"Not yet."

"I think we better get you closer before we talk about discharge." Jordan ran his fingers through his hair, which no longer had to be a buzz cut.

Squinting, Elliot asked, "I am going home, though, right?"

Jordan and Aaron exchanged an apprehensive look. "Elliot, your doctors don't know if you will be able to live independently," Aaron told him.

"Then, I'll live with you."

Jordan choked on the air he was attempting to swallow. "Dad, we love you, but no. It's not feasible."

"Why?"

"Because we like to walk around naked," Aaron said.

Before Jordan could give Aaron an altogether different kind of look, Elliot replied, "I'll leave my glasses off. It'll be fine."

How small does he think we are? "Let's take it one step at a time. We're going to do our best to keep you in your home as long as possible," Jordan said. *Please, don't bring up the fact that I'll be starting my doctorate soon and Aaron works at home. I already feel guilty enough.*

"Yes, one step at a time." Elliot focused on the television. "You two probably need rest. I'll see you when it's convenient."

"Dad…" Jordan tried, but an invisible shield now surrounded his father. "We'll come by soon."

"Hey," Aaron said once they were in the elevator, "you were honest with him. It isn't feasible in the long term. Hopefully we can afford a full-time nurse with the money the government gives us for compensation."

"Or I could postpone my PhD and take care of him. He took care of me all those years…and I wasn't even his…"

Aaron's gaze cut through Jordan's self-pity. "I am so close to going back up there and letting him respond in whatever way he deems appropriate to that remark, but you hurt enough, and I may want that ass for something. You have never doubted who your father was. Now would be a horrible time to start. We will find a solution that makes sense for all of us."

Jordan offered a smile as he hailed a cab. "Yes, sir."

THE NEXT DAY, Aaron cuddled up to Jordan on the hotel bed. Jordan wrapped his arms around him and kissed his lips. "We should have more days like this."

"Yes, weekly." Aaron nuzzled his bare chest.

They had been naked since they arrived in the hotel after picking up Jordan's car. Never had Jordan concentrated so hard not to see a place as he had not to catch sight of his house. Would he ever be able to live there without thinking back to what happened? Or, worse, what almost did? Jordan bent down and kissed Aaron's stitches. "Love you."

"Love you too." Aaron sighed. "Stop thinking about it, please."

"That would be a great trick. Can you tell me how to stop thinking about the thing that won't leave my mind?" Jordan scratched circles on his back. "The question will not leave me alone."

"What question?"

"What if? What if I had been a few moments later? What if I had hit a red light? What if someone had hit me on the way home? On the flip side, what if I had left five minutes earlier? He wouldn't have hurt you at all." Jordan pulled in shaky breaths.

"I have one more." Aaron waited for Jordan to meet his gaze. "What if you forgave yourself for not predicting the exact best moment to act? What if you accepted that even heroes can't do it all? Could you handle the knowledge that because you did act, without thinking, debating, or hesitating, the cut on my neck required ten stitches and not a wood box?" Aaron held him close.

Jordan savored his husband's scent with each inhale. The heat of their skin-to-skin contact warmed Jordan's core. He needed no more proof that he was lucky than the man in his arms. Their lips touched again, lingering this time. "Angel?"

"Hmm?"

"Did you get lube on your trip to the drugstore?" Jordan asked.

"Of course, I did. I said I was going for emergency supplies, didn't I?" Aaron jumped up and retrieved the Rite-Aid bag while Jordan chuckled.

"Most people wouldn't classify that as an emergency supply."

Aaron shrugged and lay on his back. "Most people don't have a husband they can't get enough of. Their problem, not mine. Think we should redefine the word emergency."

Jordan leaned down and kissed from his lips to his navel. "Yeah? What else would you include?"

"Oh," Aaron moaned. "Depends on our moods. Definitely lube, maybe witch hazel." He vibrated under Jordan's mouth as his kisses turned to bites.

Jordan squirted lube on both of them. He smiled as he hiked up Aaron's legs and entered him. "No need for witch hazel today. I have no desire to be rough." They worked a slow rhythm for what felt like a beautiful eternity. The white cream climaxed their fears and satiated each other.

After cleaning up, Aaron took his place on Jordan's chest again and asked, "Did you make any progress on those pro-con lists for schools?"

"Since you didn't care where we lived, I was leaning toward Stanford," Jordan responded. "But with my dad's stroke, I don't think we can be so far away."

Aaron quieted for a moment. "Why couldn't we find him an apartment close by us out there? I hear Stanford has visiting nurses associations."

"Unless he needs more than that."

"Then they also have assisted living facilities. We can research the options. One positive is that we have some money, so a cross-country move is more feasible," Aaron commented. "But...we don't need all of it, do we?"

"Of course not. Did you have a charity in mind?"

"It's going to sound really strange," Aaron started.

"I am not donating to Focus on the Family."

Aaron stared at him. "You have done the impossible. I don't even have sarcasm for that." He shook his head. "Troy was a despicable human being, but he had a ten-year-old daughter who did nothing to deserve the loss of her father, which at the very least took away her means of support. Would you be all right with setting up an anonymous trust fund for her? I won't do it if you're uncomfortable with it," he added quickly.

Jordan's heart warmed as he listened. He tilted Aaron's chin up and brushed their lips together. "You amaze me with the ways you earn your nickname." He kissed Aaron again. "Yes, we'll talk to the lawyer." He lifted his finger with the ringing of his phone.

"No," Aaron protested. "Ignore it."

"You know I can't," Jordan responded. "It's Bryant."

"Glad we didn't go too far."

"Hello?" Jordan said into the phone.

"Captain, I'm sorry to bother you on your vacation."

"It's fine, sir. What can I help you with?"

"First of all, I wanted to congratulate Aaron on identifying Jalalabad's location. He is being taken care of at Walter Reed."

"I'm relieved to hear that." After the superior officer paused for longer than necessary, Jordan prompted, "Was there anything more?"

"Yes, um, Adeela Nadar seems to be under the impression that you will be joining us on the mission...and she won't offer any more assistance without speaking to you."

Did I tell her that? Jordan wondered. *Shit.* "Do you need me to come in?"

"Would it be too much trouble?" Bryant asked.

Aaron rolled his eyes.

"No, but Aaron will be joining me."

A pause and a sigh on the other end of the phone. "That will be fine, Captain. Thank you."

Following another kiss, Jordan shed the covers and stood to dress in the jeans and button-down shirt he'd bought yesterday for just this occasion.

"Jor?" Aaron pulled on clothes.

"Yes, Angel?"

"If you must go, and I would prefer you find another way, then I'm going too." Aaron tied his shoes as he spoke.

"I might not have control over that."

"You have control over what *you* do. And that will include me." Aaron looked him in the eye. "We've had too many brushes with death in the last few months to face the possibility worlds apart. Tell me the promise you made to me when you came home—that I would never have to sit around praying to a god I don't even believe in that you're safe—is the most important thing to you. Assure me before we go over there that it ranks higher than the promises you've made to the army and Adeela. I need to hear it from you."

Jordan stared at him. He had plenty of rebuttals. Adeela had saved his life; the army could force the issue. But Aaron's words rang with truth and love. "I promise, Angel."

Aaron smiled and kissed him. "Thank you."

Chapter Thirty-Four

I AM SURROUNDED by stubborn people who spend way too much time being right, Jordan griped to himself as he waited at ready in the secret American army base, a quarter mile from the prison he'd been trapped in. As predicted, Adeela refused to trust anyone except Jordan to free her. She had informed Bryant that, no, she would not blindly place her life in his hands. When asked why, she cited his recent track record, but the United States needed her knowledge and proximity to enemy forces. Jordan agreed to assist, which turned to lead. Therefore, Aaron stood across the room discussing enemy movement with Colonel Bryant. Jordan smiled in spite of his annoyance. Aaron was hot when he got impassioned, which he had been quite a lot lately.

"All clear," Bryant called, yanking Jordan from his daydream about Aaron's ass.

Bad thing to think about now anyway.

"Captain, confirm with Adeela," Bryant directed.

Jordan sent a text message.

Ready for us?

Her response was immediate.

Yes. Anwar is quiet.

Quiet... Jordan flashed back to the day he woke up to find the Afghanistan government had taken him prisoner. *Dead prisoners are too quiet.*

"She's ready."

Bryant pointed to the door. "Move out then."

Aaron gave Jordan a nod of encouragement. *No time for long goodbyes.* Jordan led the five men backing him on the mission out of the underground base. The only sound in the night air was the tread of the soldiers' boots on the sand. The night before, they had planted several IEDs around the building, which would be activated once Adeela and the Afghan prisoners were safe. They chose the night so Adeela had the best chance of leaving unnoticed, but why was her husband dead? The American soldiers on guard had reported no unrest between him and his guards. "Have we spoken to the soldiers staking out the prison?" Jordan asked the man behind him.

"Yes, sir, been a very uneventful day," he replied. "No one has gone in or out."

"Keep alert, Sergeant."

Jordan pressed the call button on his headset as they neared the prison. Adeela answered on the second ring. "Where are you?"

"Admissions," she responded. "All is clear."

"We'll be there in less than a minute." He ended the call to keep all his senses on guard for an attack as they approached, but no guards blocked the entrance. "Draw your guns." Jordan noted six guns leaving their holsters as the men followed him through the stone entranceway. He turned on the light on the end of his gun and used it to guide them across the dirty floor toward the admissions office.

"I'm alone, Jordan," Adeela said.

Jordan's heart pounded as he lowered his weapon and stepped into the office to find Adeela sitting on top of the desk, gun at her side, and blood on the walls. Nadar's blood. The man lay lifeless on the floor. "Where are the guards?"

"Quiet in the back." Adeela was more relaxed than he expected. Almost...detached.

"Two of you, go down the hallway and confirm the status of the guards," Jordan ordered and waited while they obeyed. "Are you okay?" he asked her.

"That is one word for it," Adeela answered. She grabbed the gun by the muzzle and offered it to Jordan. He grasped the handle and dropped it in his bag.

Jordan reached his hand out to her and helped her off the desk. "You're a good shot."

Adeela gave him a faint smile. "I have lots of surprises." She dropped his hand as they left the office.

"Why aren't you carrying her?" a soldier asked Jordan.

"If I can shoot and kill four men, I should have no trouble walking out of a building on my own," Adeela replied.

"She isn't injured. We need cleanup crew," he told the man. "Did you free the prisoners?" he asked Adeela.

"No. They are guilty. I did not kill them if that is your next question."

"But they're quiet," the soldier protested.

Adeela turned to him. "You would be if you saw your meek nurse kill the men who struck you with terror for years."

The rest of the soldiers stifled their laughter. "Report back to Colonel Bryant," Jordan instructed. As one of them did, he turned to Adeela again. "What did you need us for?"

"Immunity." Adeela cringed. "May we leave? This place smells like death."

Jordan nodded and led her and one of the soldiers to the base while the rest coordinated the cleanup. Upon entering, Aaron threw himself into Jordan's arms. Jordan laughed. "Angel, that was the least dangerous rescue mission ever."

"I'm fine with that," Aaron replied.

"You didn't confront Nadar?" Bryant asked.

"Didn't need to." Jordan motioned Adeela forward. "Adeela, this is Colonel Bryant."

"Pleasure, Khanum Nadar." The lieutenant colonel bowed his head.

"And you as well, Colonel. It was unnecessary for Jordan to kill Anwar because I had already taken care of him and his friends. The only people left alive are the prisoners and the American soldiers," Adeela informed him.

"You...killed your husband? There was no battle? The only Afghan people left alive are those who pose no real threat to us?"

"Yes. Does the lack of explosives disappoint you?"

"Um, no..." the lieutenant colonel stuttered.

Aaron buried his face in Jordan's neck to quell his laughter. The correct answer was yes, it took a lot of money and planning to coordinate the placement of those explosives. So, it would be a shame not to see them used. "Should we let the Afghan government know about the murders?" Jordan asked.

"Will you take credit for them, please?" Adeela requested.

"Adeela, that is never a problem," Aaron answered. "Our military is glad to take the credit for any heroic acts."

"Doesn't he exhaust you, Captain?" Colonel Bryant sighed.

Jordan started laughing. "Yes, sir, he does. Every day of my life." He glanced at Aaron. "No, don't say it."

"Not saying a thing," Aaron replied.

Chapter Thirty-Five

FORTY-EIGHT HOURS later, they stepped onto American soil. Bryant had told them repeatedly how sorry he was to sign Jordan's discharge papers, but Aaron did not share his sentiments.

Adeela had been quiet, only speaking when asked a question. The United States government had promised her full citizenship and sixty days in government housing. "What am I supposed to do after sixty days? Do you think American hospitals are going to be jumping to hire an Afghan nurse whose experience mostly came from working in a prison?" she asked Jordan and Aaron when they were alone in her hospital room at Walter Reed, where the government insisted she receive a battery of tests.

"You can use those sixty days to take the tests required to..." Aaron smiled as an idea formed.

"Oh, no," Jordan said.

"What?" Adeela glanced between them.

"He's smiling."

"How is that bad?"

Jordan lifted one corner of his mouth. "Unless you can tell me what he has to smile *about*, it isn't necessarily good."

Aaron tried to scowl at him, but the energy from his epiphany prevented the annoyance from sticking. "You're right, Adeela. It may be difficult to find a job in a hospital so quickly, but I may have an alternative for you."

"What is that?"

His grin widened. "Can you handle stubborn patients?"

Adeela laughed. "I handled him, didn't I?" She gestured to Jordan, and Aaron joined in her laughter.

"You did. Now, imagine Jordan's stubbornness in a seventy-five-year-old stroke patient."

Finally, Jordan smiled, reached over, and grasped his hand.

They spent the next four hours filling her in on the plans for their move and Elliot's condition, at which point the doctor kicked them out to allow Adeela to rest.

Once they entered Elliot's room, Aaron blinked at his brother sitting in a chair. "Chris, what are you doing here?"

"Keeping Elliot company while you two prevent terrorist attacks," he replied.

"You should have gotten more recognition for your part in it," Elliot added.

Jordan sat down. "We declined the medals of honor. You always told me not to get into the military for glory. We did what we did because it was right."

Elliot glowed with a pride Aaron hadn't seen in a while.

While Jordan told Elliot about their plans, Aaron walked out into the hallway with Chris.

"You're leaving for good?" Chris asked.

"Good or bad, we'll see."

"Will you visit Dad before you leave? He's been trying to call you."

"No. What he said when Jordan was gone... Unforgivable."

"We all said—"

"Chris, don't."

Chris nodded. "I really respect your ability to move on with your life after all the shit that's been thrown at you."

Aaron didn't understand what was commendable about surviving. "Thanks," he said anyway.

"I've had the same job for three months," Chris stated.

"That's a start. Do you like it?" Aaron asked.

"It…pays the bills, not as exciting as yours."

"I am more than ready to be boring."

"Your life could never be boring." Chris released a breath. "Can I visit?"

Aaron smiled. "Sure. When you've been employed for a year, we'll celebrate by going skydiving."

THE DAY OF Adeela's discharge coincided with that of Jalalabad's. He had a seat on a flight to Afghanistan the next morning.

"Adeela, would you like to see Imam Jalalabad before he leaves?" Jordan asked.

"I thought he was under constant protection."

"He is, but I talked some people into clearing you."

Adeela fingered the bedsheet. "I do not know if he would want to see me after what I have done to his people."

"He does," Jordan spoke softly. "He made the request."

She raised her gaze, infused again with fierceness. "Then please take me to him." Adeela adjusted her hijab and followed Jordan out of the room with her shoulders back. He wasn't sure if she was happy or steeling herself for a battle, but the idea that the imam had called for her increased her confidence.

Jordan led her to his room, knocked, and walked in at the sound of his voice. "Imam Jalalabad, Adeela Nadar," he announced, bowing his head.

Adeela advanced past Jordan, met Jalalabad's eyes, and dropped to her knees, sobbing. "Please forgive me," she sputtered in Farsi.

Jalalabad placed his hand on her shoulder and replied in kind, "Be still, my child, Allah loves you."

Jordan nodded to the soldiers guarding Jalalabad's room to indicate her safety and stepped out to give them some privacy.

Epilogue

NINE MONTHS LATER

"So, let me get this straight," Adeela began as she, Aaron, Jordan, Chris, and Elliot rode down Highway 4 to Bay Area Skydiving. "Jordan, you survived multiple deployments, imprisonment by a foreign government, broken bones, and a bad case of pneumonia. And, Aaron, you lived through a home invader who intended to kill you."

"Yeah. That's right." Aaron grinned as he watched the blurred palm trees along the side of the road.

"After all of that, you want to jump out of a perfectly good airplane?"

Jordan laughed. "We've been talking about this for months, Adeela. Why are you only now getting incredulous?"

"I thought you were joking!" she answered. "Elliot, why are you allowing this?"

"Ever tried telling him no?" Elliot countered, then shrugged. "Besides, if they both die, I get their fortune."

Fortune was stretching it, but none of them had to worry about money. They were giving half of it to charity, anyway.

Elliot and Adeela had hit it off immediately. They shared passions for debating military politics and driving Jordan crazy. But Adeela's no-bullshit nature made her the perfect choice for Elliot's caregiver. With her help, he'd been regaining use of his left arm.

In the back seat, Chris protested that Elliot should not automatically get all of it, but Adeela ignored him and asked, "But after surviving all of that, why would you defy death intentionally?"

Jordan reached over and squeezed Aaron's hand. "We're skydiving because angels should fly."

After Aaron hit the radio button, Billy Joel's "You're My Home" filled the car. Aaron smiled at his husband. "Heroes too."

About the Author

Liz Borino has been telling stories of varying truthfulness since she was a child. As an adult, she keeps the fiction on the page. She writes stories of human connection and intimacy, in all their forms. Her books feature flawed men who often risk everything for their love.

When Liz isn't writing, she's waking up early to edit, travel, and explore historic prisons and insane asylums—not (usually) all in one day. Liz lives in Philadelphia with her two cats and her significant other.

Email: liz.borino@gmail.com

Other books by this author

Lucky Cowboy

Also Available from NineStar Press

Connect with NineStar Press

Website: NineStarPress.com

Facebook: NineStarPress

Facebook Reader Group: NineStarNiche

Twitter: @ninestarpress

Tumblr: NineStarPress

Without explanation, CIA officials pull Agent Aaron "Angel" Collins off a top-secret Afghanistan mission he's spent months preparing for. Due to repeated deceptions, Aaron's husband, Captain Jordan Collins, decides to retire after this deployment.

Major General Troy Hart inserts himself into Aaron's life, somehow getting past his personal barriers and better judgment. When Troy, in his capacity as a high-ranking officer, delivers some devastating news about Jordan, he becomes the only one who supports Aaron's search for the truth. Unbeknownst to Aaron, Jordan and Troy's dark history taints everything about the present.

Jordan awakens in an Afghanistan prison, beaten, ill, and fighting for his life. To get home to his Angel he must put his trust in a woman he was taught to fear.

When the mystery of Jordan's disappearance is solved, another surfaces. Jordan and Aaron's unauthorized search for the truth calls into question everything they thought they knew, until all they trust is each other. But exposing the wrong people threatens to bring their worst nightmares to fruition.